THE VICTORIAN

Act I : Self Realization

Story Created and Plotted by

Trainor Houghton

Scripts by

Lovern Kindzierski

Pencils by

Martin Montiel Luna

Inks by

Jose Carlos Buelna

Editor

Marlaine Maddux

Assistant Editor

Angelita V. Menchaca

Painted Cover by

Bob Larkin

Comic Coloring and Lettering by

Jamison Services

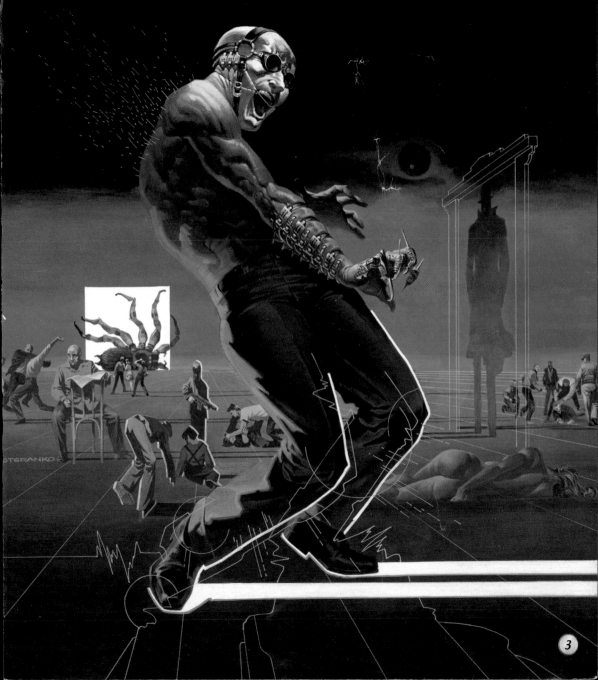

3

The Victorian — sketch by Jim Steranko

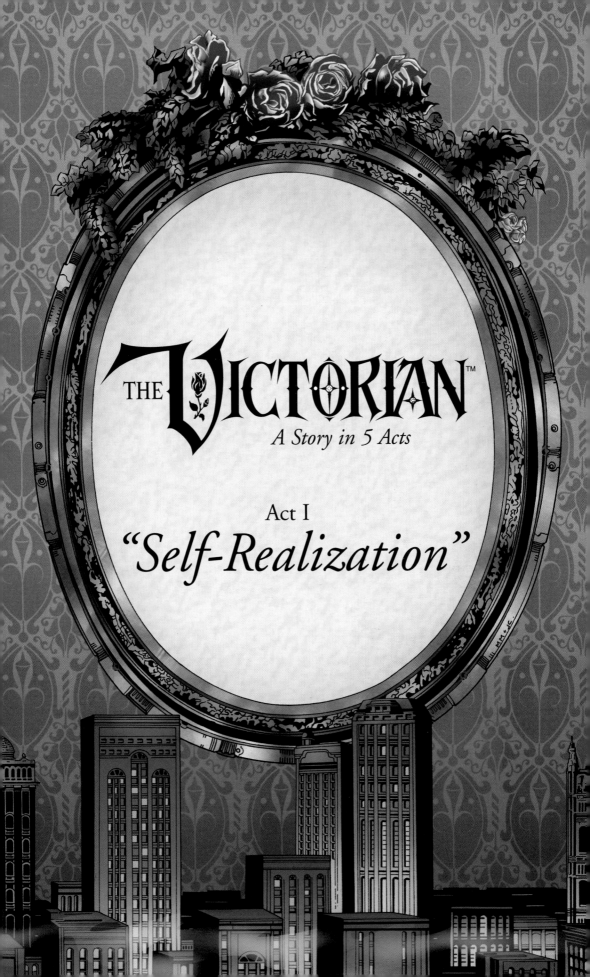

THE VICTORIAN™

A Story in 5 Acts

Act I

"Self-Realization"

RIOTS IN INDONESIA CONTINUE...

...AS WE OBSERVE THE FASCINATING ARACHNID MATING RITUAL.

YOUR TIME'S UP, STROUD. THIS IS IT, NO MORE RUNNING AWAY FROM YOURSELF. THIS IS THE END OF THE LINE.

ZZZZ

...SKYCAM FOOTAGE OF TODAY'S TERRORIST BOMBING IN ARGENTINA.

...AFTER WHICH THE BLACK WIDOW PROCEEDS TO DEVOUR THE HAPLESS MALE.

MY WORLD WAS COMING APART AND THERE WAS NO DOOR THROUGH WHICH TO ESCAPE.
WINSTONNNN

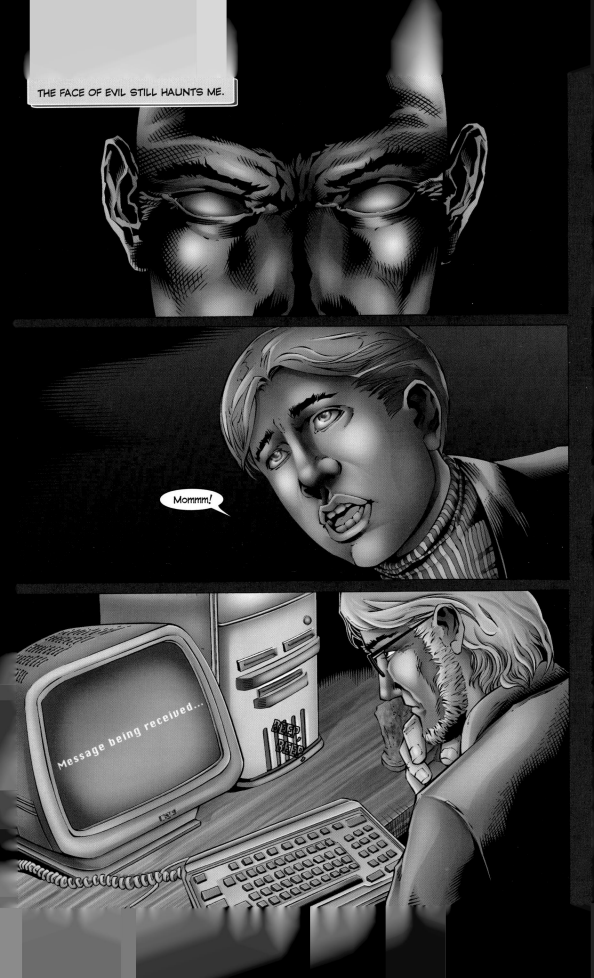

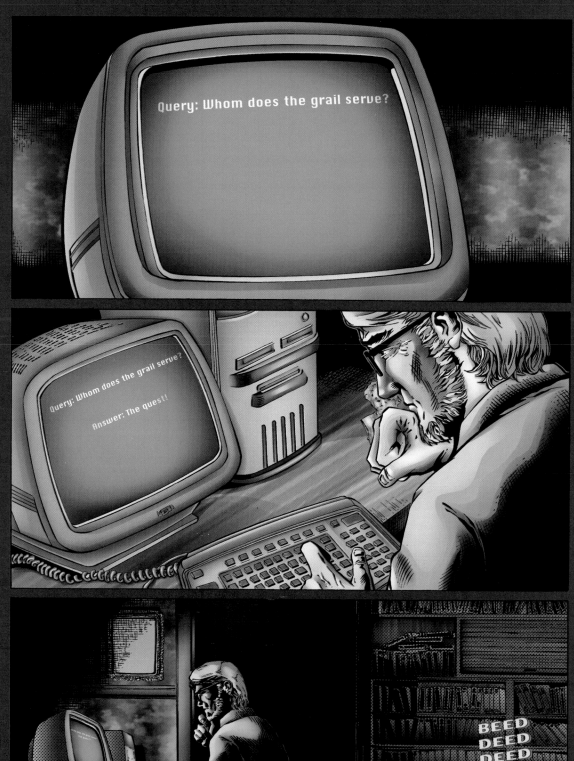

CHAPTER ONE

TOURS OF THE BLUE CLOCK

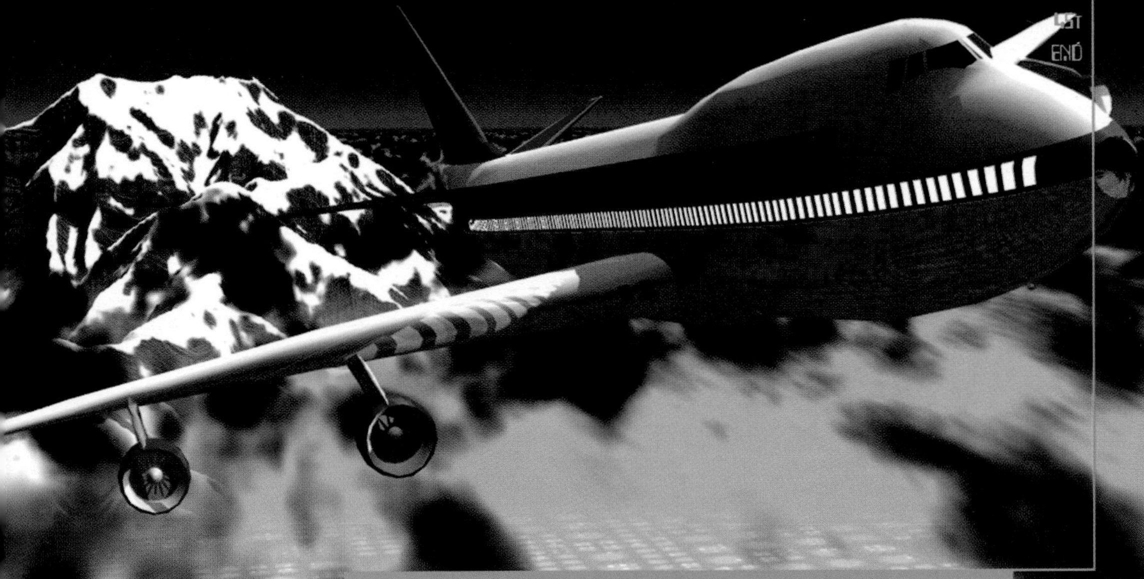

9812
YY654
87U76
O981Y
987JS
4RE
733BJE
98262
JD7083
KD7D
837J
2B27HD
923JS
2973JMX

75YU47
FG444
5654FDR
454FT
23RF
235
WE3
F345
245
23A
LST
END

"ONE CROWDED HOUR OF GLORIOUS LIFE
IS WORTH AN AGE WITHOUT A NAME."

OLD MORTALITY (1816)
- SIR WALTER SCOTT

IMPRESSIVE. ...OF COURSE.

CHEAP WATCH! I WONDER WHAT TIME IT REALLY IS?

CAN YOU DIRECT ME TO THE ROOM OF LASZLO GEREVICH?

ARE YOU FAMILY?

AS FAR AS I KNOW, HE HAS NO FAMILY.

EXPLAINS WHY HE HAS NO VISITORS.

FOLLOW ME.

THROUGH THIS DOOR. THIS IS MR. GEREVICH'S ROOM.

WHERE IS HE?

LASZLO?

And those days in Paris with Lily. Time seemed to stand still.

It felt like it would last forever.

THIS GUY'S ABOUT TO MAKE ME CRY.

CHRIST! I WONDER WHAT BIG "O" THINKS WE'LL LEARN FROM THIS?

She was the picture of youth and innocence, but her passion was unforgettable.

My memories are an odd mix of past and present.

Paris was magical in those days. On our last night together, Lily and I saw the great actor, Coquelin, in his sensational portrayal of Cyrano.

ROARRR!

CLAP!

CLAP!

We danced all night in the shadow of the great Eiffel tower that was not yet complete.

FITZ, DO YOU SUPPOSE IT WAS REALLY THAT PERFECT, OR ARE THESE THE TRICKS PLAYED BY AN OLD MAN'S MEMORIES?

WHAT DIFFERENCE DOES IT MAKE, OLD FRIEND, IT'S THE WAY YOU BELIEVE IT WAS.

FITZ, YOU LOOK DISTRACTED. AM I BEGINNING TO RAMBLE?

NO, NOT AT ALL. I ENJOY PICTURING YOU IN THOSE DAYS. I'M HONORED THAT YOU'RE SHARING THESE MEMORIES.

SEE IF YOU CAN RAISE THE BIG "O". SOUNDS LIKE HE'S GOING TO BE IN THERE FOR AWHILE. SHOULD WE WAIT FOR THE CLOCK TO MOVE AGAIN?

I shared my last hours in Paris with statues that appeared more melancholy than myself.

The angel's wings had fallen, stone on stone.

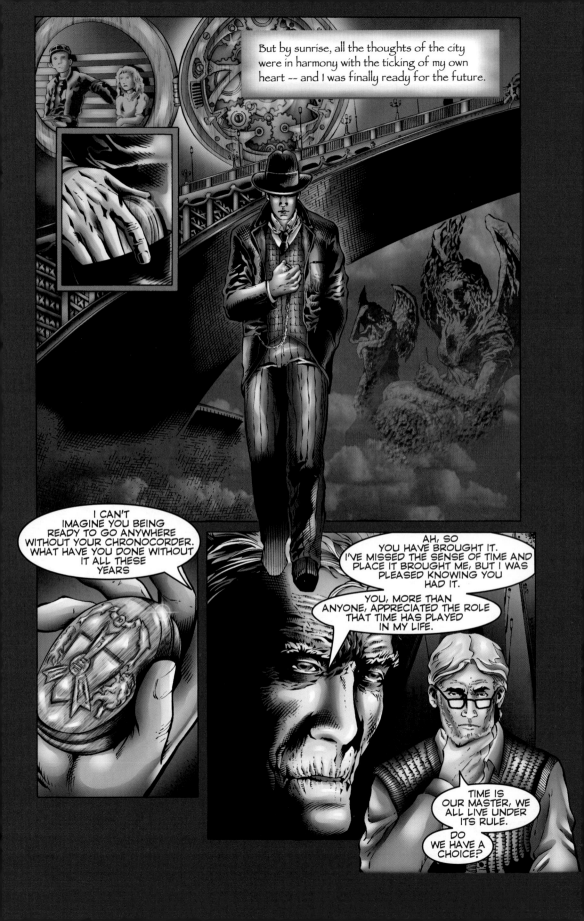

There are some who believe we do.

THE GAME IS AFOOT!

Closing Hour by Keith Martin and Rober Quijan

CITY OF DRE

DALLAS, TEXAS
NOVEMBER 21, 1963

DFUL NIGHT

Fitz, did you relate to the feeling
of isolation in the poem,

KRAK-THOooMMM

AH YES, JAMES THOMSON. ...HE, MORE THAN ANYONE, CAPTURED THAT ERA'S SENSE OF FRACTURED IDENTITY.

WINSTON, MAYBE YOU'LL SEE SOMETHING YOU WANT FOR CHRISTMAS.

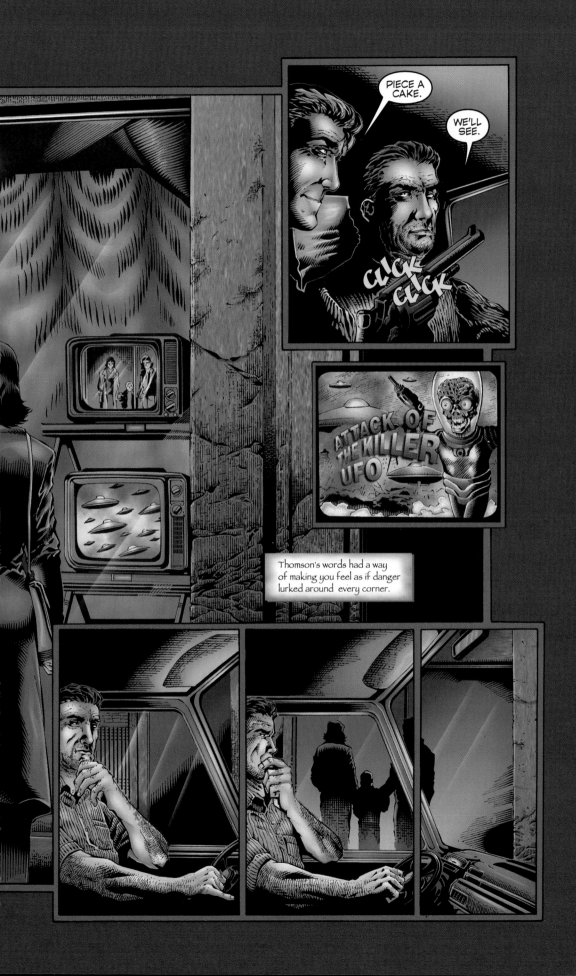

PLEASE, NO!

TAKE 'EM!

HA HA HA HA HA HA HA HA HA HA

DON'T MAKE A SOUND KID, OR I'LL BLOW YOUR HEAD OFF!

AAUGH!

ESCAPE IS IMPOSSIBLE, ACCEPT YOUR FATE.

It was a philosophy that served me well for a time.

NOOOOOOOOOOOOOOOOOOOO···

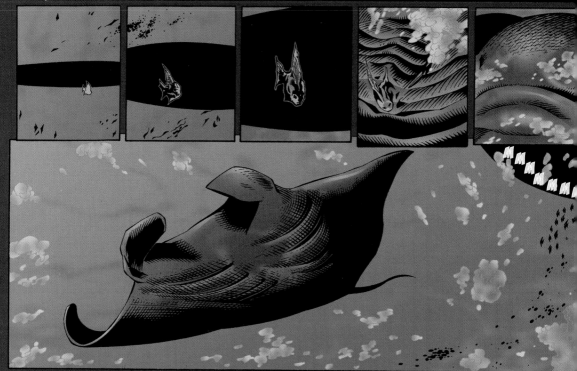

NORWEGIAN SEA
100 MILES OFF THE COAST OF THE
FAEROE ISLANDS
APRIL 20, 1999

HMS STORMBRINGER
 CLASS: VANGUARD SSBN (BATCH II)
 DISPLACEMENT: 36,000 (DIVED)
 DIMENSIONS: LENGTH: 670.9/206
   BEAM: 98.8/43
   DAFT: 65/17.4
 MACHINERY: 2 PWR-2 POWER PLANT
 2-PUMPJET PROPULSOR - 90,000 SHP
 SPEED: CLASSIFIED
 (BELIEVED TO EXCEED 36 KNOTS DIVED)
 USERS: UNITED KINGDOM

BAD STORM'S BREWIN'. I CAN SMELL IT.

METEOROLOGY INDICATES WE'RE SAILING RIGHT INTO THE TEETH OF IT.

HAND ME THE BINOCULARS.

TELL THE OFFICER OF THE DECK TO PREPARE TO DIVE.

AYE, AYE, SIR.

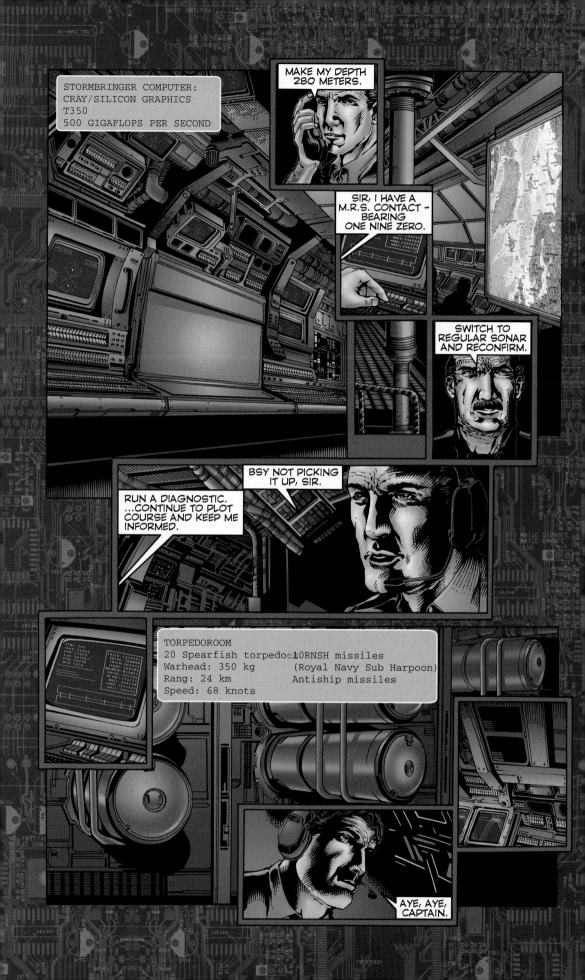

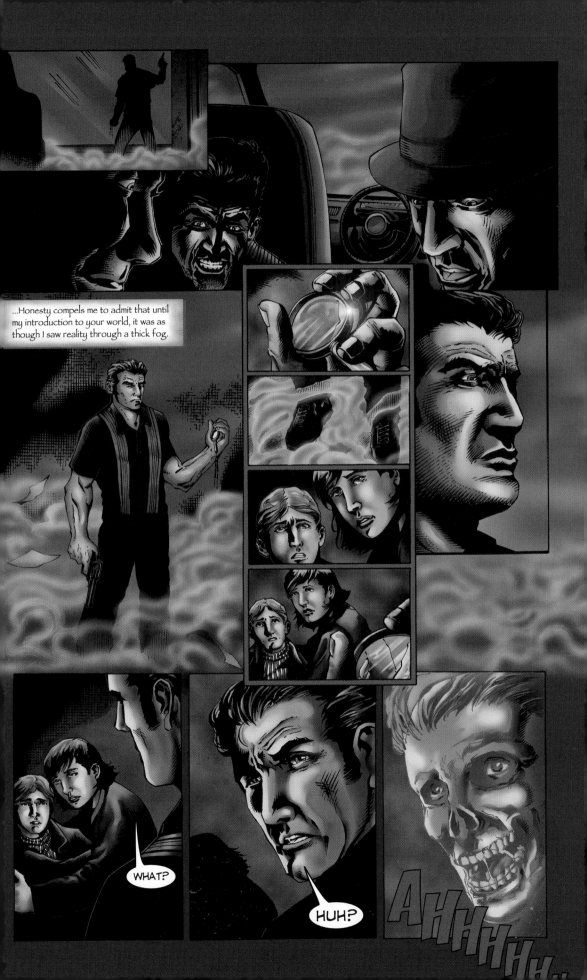

...Honesty compels me to admit that until my introduction to your world, it was as though I saw reality through a thick fog.

WHAT?

HUH?

AHHHHHH...

HHHHHHBEEP BEEP
CLICK
CLICK
OBJECT 200 METERS OFF STARBOARD BOW.
EEET
EEESHHHHHHH
COME LEFT TO COURSE TWO, TWO, ZERO AND BEGIN EVASIVE MANEUVERS.
BREAK RADIO SILENCE AND CONTACT NAVAL OPERATIONS.
EEESHHHHHHH
OBJECT CLOSING FAST!

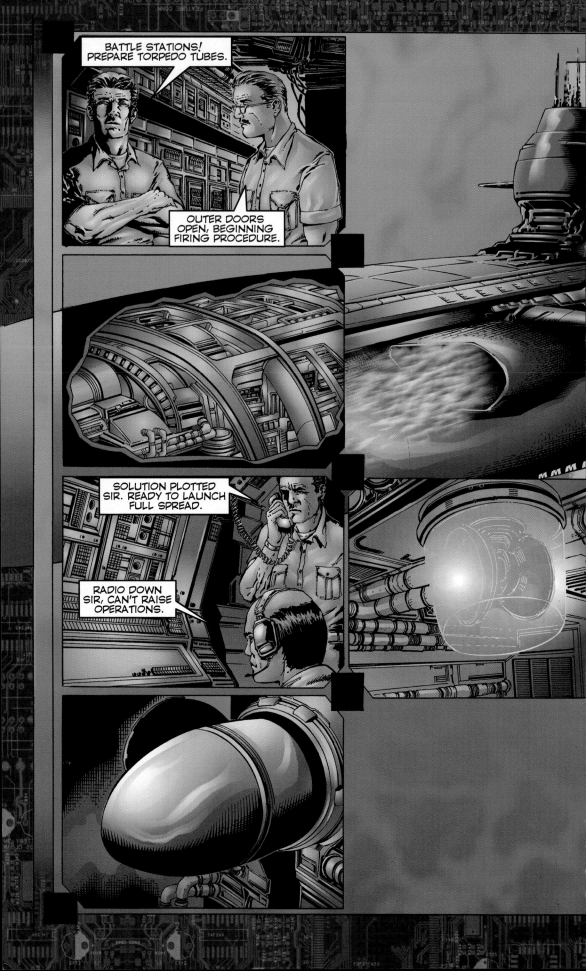

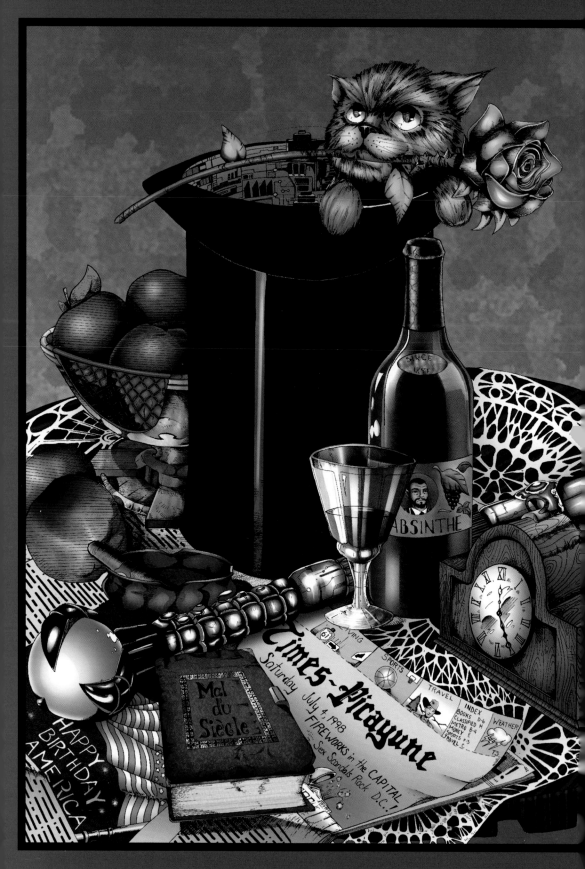

Cat in the Hat by Courtney Huddleston

Chapter Three
Terminal Deep

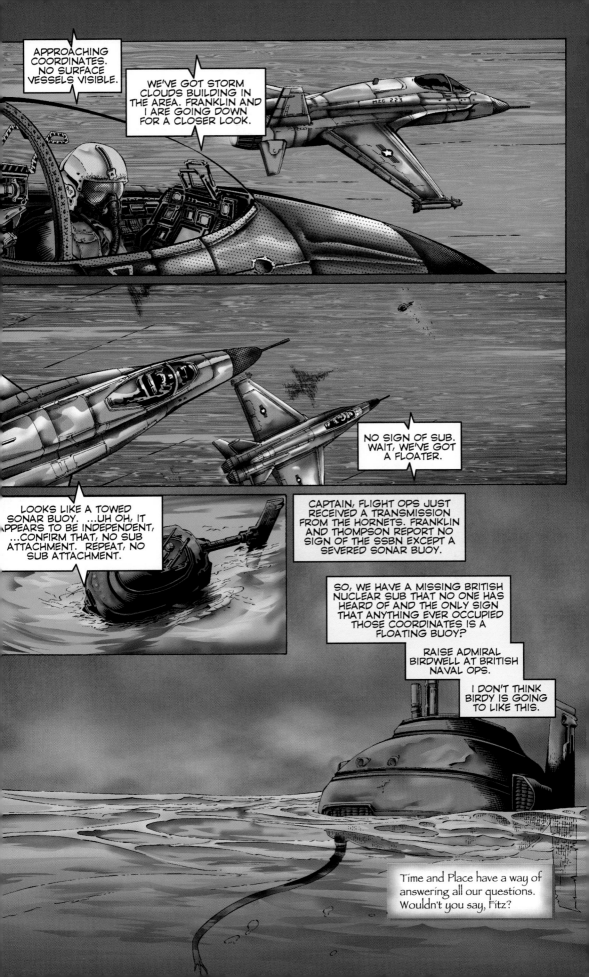

THE FINAL FAREWELL.

I SUPPOSE... BUT OFTEN, TIME HAS A WAY OF MOVING VERY SLOWLY.

FOR ME THAT ONLY SEEMS TRUE WHEN I READ THOMSON'S *CITY OF DREADFUL NIGHT*. HIS POEM AND PARIS HAVE BEEN MUCH ON MY MIND OF LATE.

ARE YOU THINKING OF LILY?

MOSTLY REMEMBERING THAT AFTER THOSE LAST FEW DAYS IN FRANCE, THERE WAS NO TIME TO MOURN FOR HER.

Even before I returned to London, the *Society* had planned my final mission.

It was an assignment whose very success sealed my fate and allowed no turning back.

OUR ADVENTURES MUST HAVE BEEN PALE COMPARED TO YOUR LIFE IN THOSE DAYS.

ON THE CONTRARY... I LEARNED MORE IN THAT SHORT TIME THAN IN THE INTELLECTUAL AND PRIVILEGED EMBRACE OF THE SECRET SOCIETY.

IT WAS AS IF THOSE EARLY YEARS WERE PREPARATION, AND MY TIME HERE WAS REALIZATION.

DO YOU THINK THAT WAS ALSO TRUE OF BALLARÉ? HE HAD MANY YEARS TO USE THE CYCLOCHRONOMETER AND PERFECT HIS SCHEME. WITH AN UNDERSTANDING OF UNIVERSAL TIME AND OF SOCIAL VULNERABILITY, HE HAD AN ADVANTAGE OVER ALL OTHERS.

YES, A RENEGADE SCHEME THAT STRUCK TERROR AND REMORSE IN THE HEARTS OF MY MENTORS AND SET THE COURSE OF MY DESTINY.

OUR DESTINIES BROUGHT US TOGETHER, OLD FRIEND, AND I WILL ALWAYS BE GRATEFUL FOR THOSE DAYS.

I WANT TO LEAVE YOU THE MANUSCRIPT THAT HAS TAKEN ME FOUR YEARS TO COMPLETE. I NEVER EXPECTED TO BE ABLE TO SHARE IT WITH YOU. ...YET YOU ARE THE ONLY PERSON WHO WILL FULLY UNDERSTAND IT.

WHAT AN IRONY, FITZ. I TOO, HAVE A BOOK FOR YOU. I HAVE RECORDED MY FINAL THOUGHTS BETWEEN ITS COVERS AND IT IS TIME FOR ME TO MOVE ON.

OH YES, I REMEMBER THIS. HOW OFTEN HAVE I SEEN YOU SCRIBBLE ON THESE PAGES? I WAS ALWAYS INTRIGUED BY HOW THIS SIMPLE ACT WOULD STEADY YOU.

I NEVER IMAGINED THAT I WOULD BE PRIVY TO ITS CONTENTS. I ALWAYS KNEW IT WAS TERRITORY MUCH TOO PERSONAL FOR ME TO INVADE. I FEEL HUMBLED BY THIS HONOR.

CONTACT BIG "O". THIS MEETING IS WINDING DOWN. DO WE STAY WITH THE CLOCK OR WRAP IT UP? THERE ISN'T MUCH HERE. I'M AFRAID THE TRAIL IS TOO COLD. HAVE I-COM RUN A CHECK ON THE NAME BALLARÉ. LET'S SEE WHAT WE TURN UP.

READ MY BOOK IN THOSE QUIET MOMENTS

WHEN YOU THINK OF ME.

SLEEP WELL, OLD FRIEND. I WILL ALWAYS REMEMBER.

DALLAS, TEXAS
NOVEMBER 21, 1963

SKHHHKHH

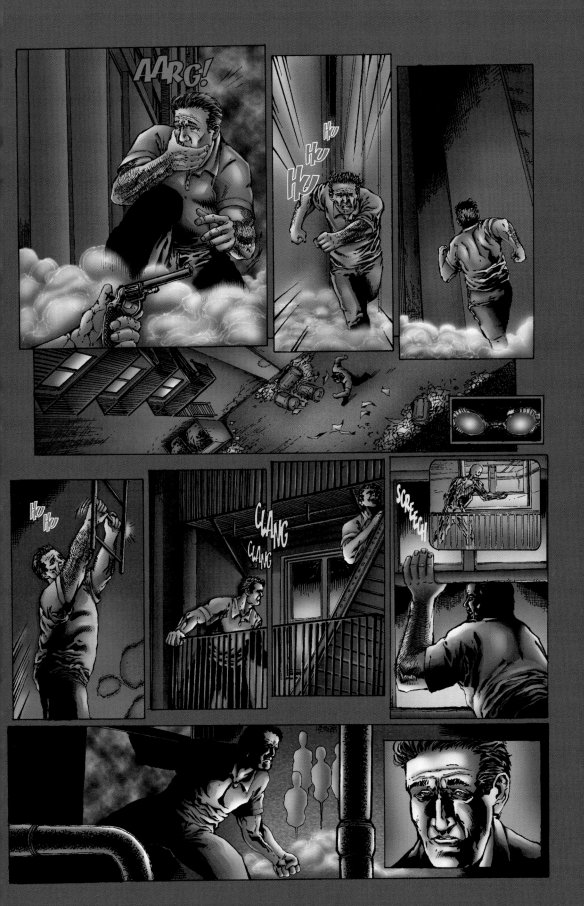

LOCALLY, STUDENTS AT AMHERST COLLEGE GATHERED AT CAMPUS CENTER YESTERDAY TO SIGN A PETITION PROTESTING THE SCHOOL'S TENURE POLICIES. SCHOOL OFFICIALS DECLINED TO COMMENT.

CLICK

IN NATIONAL NEWS, MARINE BIOLOGISTS ARE SCRATCHING THEIR HEADS OVER THE SIGHTING OF NUMEROUS HAMMERHEAD SHARKS IN THE MISSISSIPPI DELTA REGION OF NEW ORLEANS. WHILE THE STRANGE IS CONSIDERED COMMONPLACE IN NEW ORLEANS, THIS REPORT HAS THEM STUMPED.

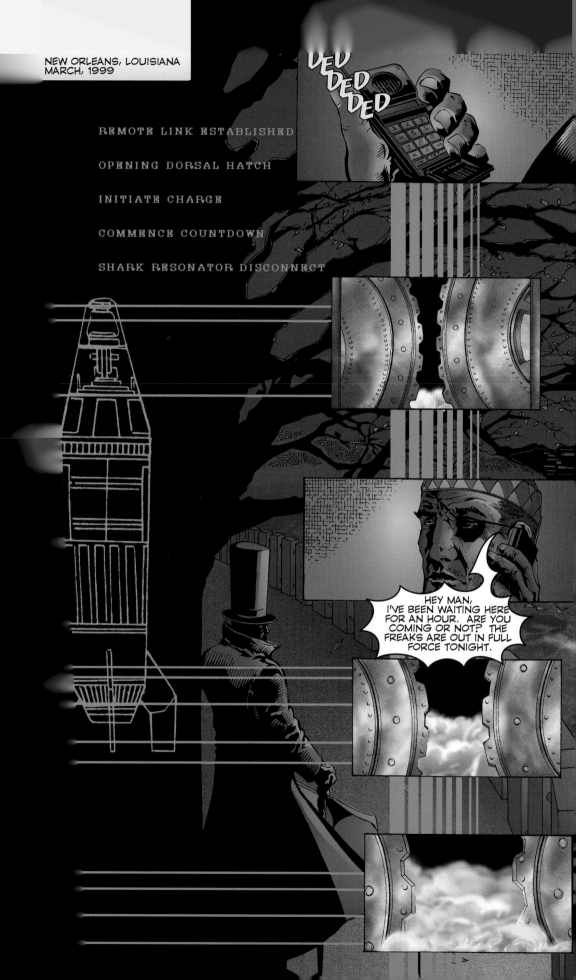

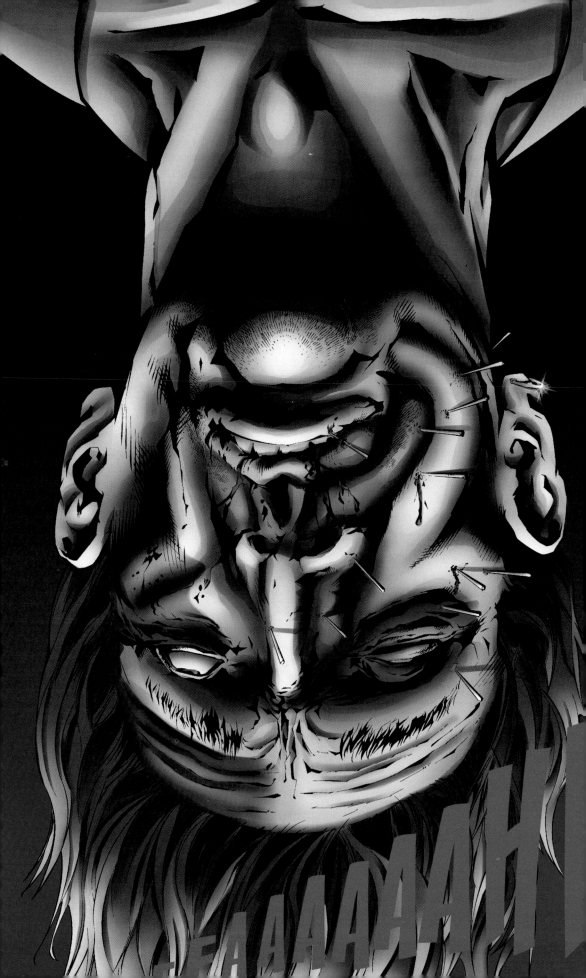

CHAPTER 4
Something Wakes on the Wind

Though now but marble are the marble urns,
Though fountains droop in waning light and pain
Glitters on the edges of wet ferns,
I should not dare to let you in again.

Mine is a world foregone though not yet ended,--
An imagined garden grey with sundered boughs
And broken branches, wistful and unmended,
And mist that is more constant than all vows.

Postcript
Hart Crane

ELIZABETH. YOU HEAR ME CHERE? OR ARE YOU AND MARIE LAVEAU'S DAUGHTER COOKING UP A ROUX FOR SOME BON GUMBO? BESS, YOU DON'T LET THAT PIRATE CAPTAIN YOU TURN YOUR HEAD, GIRL. YOU REMEMBER YOU'RE A MARRIED WOMAN.

I KNOW I OWE YOU AN APOLOGY - NOT COMING 'ROUND FOR SO LONG . . . NEARLY A MONTH NOW. BUT A LOT OF THINGS BEEN HAPPENING, BESS. LOTS OF VOODOO "PETRO" CRAP GOING ON OUT HERE. YOU JUST ASK MARIE II.

BET THAT "MAMBO" KNOWS ALL ABOUT THAT SHRINE WE FOUND . . . SEEMS LIKE YESTERDAY KELLER AND I GOT CALLED TO THE ASSAULT SCENE.

ST. LOUIS NO. 2 CEMETERY "CITY OF THE DEAD".
THE PROBLEM AROSE IN THOSE EARLIEST DAYS OF THE FRENCH COLONY OF HOW TO BURY THE DEAD IN A PLACE SO MARSHY THAT A COFFIN WOULD FLOAT TO THE SURFACE IN THE FIRST RAINSTORM. THE ANSWER IN BELOW-SEA-LEVEL NEW ORLEANS WAS ABOVE-GROUND INTERMENT.

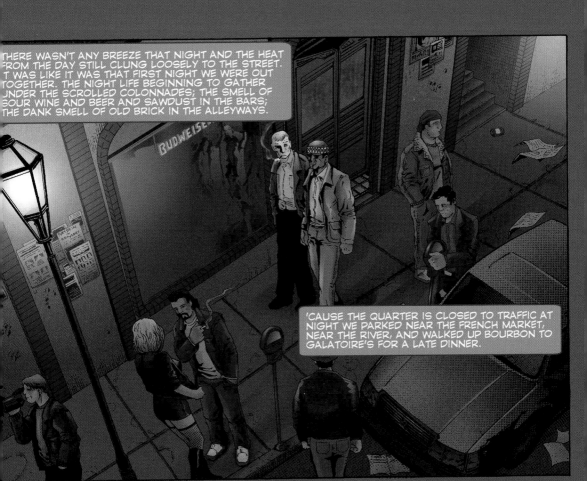

THERE WASN'T ANY BREEZE THAT NIGHT AND THE HEAT FROM THE DAY STILL CLUNG LOOSELY TO THE STREET. T. WAS LIKE IT WAS THAT FIRST NIGHT WE WERE OUT TOGETHER. THE NIGHT LIFE BEGINNING TO GATHER UNDER THE SCROLLED COLONNADES; THE SMELL OF SOUR WINE AND BEER AND SAWDUST IN THE BARS; THE DANK SMELL OF OLD BRICK IN THE ALLEYWAYS.

'CAUSE THE QUARTER IS CLOSED TO TRAFFIC AT NIGHT WE PARKED NEAR THE FRENCH MARKET, NEAR THE RIVER, AND WALKED UP BOURBON TO GALATOIRE'S FOR A LATE DINNER.

KELLER WAS SOUNDING OFF ABOUT SAIGON AGAIN, LIKE HE WAS THE ONLY ONE WHO HAD DISCOVERED SOME DARK TRUTH ABOUT THE WORLD IN VIET NAM.

I'M TELLIN' YOU, BIG EASY IS JUST LIKE SAIGON BEFORE THE FALL, MAN.

MY FAVORITE BUNCH OF HUSTLERS WERE OUT IN FORCE. DANCING TO THE MUSIC FROM THE BARS, THEIR CLIP-ON TAPS RINGING LIKE HORSESHOES ON THE CONCRETE.

YOU DON'T THINK ONE OF THESE LITTLE SCAM ARTISTS WOULDN'T *FRAG* YOU FOR SOME OF THE COLOMBIANS' LONG GREEN?

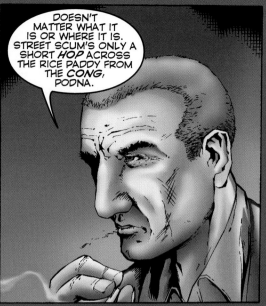

HEY KELLER MAN, SPECIAL FORCES - IS THAT LIKE - THE SPECIAL OLYMPICS?

CUT THE CRAP HARRIMAN!

TOO RIGHT, RAY. YOU ASKED FOR OUR HELP SO LET'S GET TO WORK.

NIGHT WATCHMAN CALLED IN WHEN HE FOUND THE BODIES ON HIS ROUNDS. UNIFORMS CAME DOWN AND FOUND THE SHRINE.

SCORE ONE FOR THE NIGHT WATCH!

SO HOW'D YOU KNOW IT WAS A PRO WHO DID THEM?

READ THE STORY, LEVITICUS, IT'S WRITTEN ALL OVER THE FLOOR . . . AND THE WALL . . . AND THE CEILING.

KELLER?

IT WAS ONE GUY. LOOKS LIKE HE WAS UNARMED, USED THEIR OWN GUNS AGAINST THEM. JUDGING BY THE SCUFF MARKS AND BLOOD SPRAY PATTERNS I'D SAY HE WAS PLAYING WITH THEM. THE WAY HE STRUNG THEM UP . . . TEACHING THEM A LESSON.

KELLER, MAN. YOU ARE THE SPOOK'S SPOOK.

YOU READ TOO MUCH LECARRE, BS.

YOUR TURN, LEVITICUS.

SO,
WHATTA YOU
MAKE OF
THIS?

TRY NOT TO MESS ANYTHING, DOC. THE CRIME SCENE GUYS HAVEN'T BEEN HERE YET. SOME GREASEBALL AND HIS MUSCLE GOT WASTED BY SOME UNIFORMS AND CRIME SCENE IS HUNG UP THERE.

SEE THOSE HALOGENS. THIS PLACE AIN'T WHAT IT SEEMS.

YEAH. USUALLY A SHRINE LIKE THIS HAS A WHOLE TEMPLE BUILT AROUND IT.

YOU SAYIN' THIS AIN'T VOODOO?

I DON'T KNOW IF IT IS, RAY, AND THAT LEADS ME TO BELIEVE THAT IT'S NOT.

ELEMENTARY, MY DEAR WATSON.

B.S.!

IT WAS MORE AN EXPRESSION OF SOMETHING THAN A MONUMENT.

I MEAN, IT HAD EVERYTHING THAT ANY SHRINE I'VE EVER SEEN HAD, BUT . . . IT WAS DIFFERENT, BESS.

FOR ONE THING IT DIDN'T SEEM TO BE DEDICATED TO ANY LOA.

IT REMINDED ME OF THAT INSTALLATION AT THAT ART SHOW WE SAW. YOU KNOW, THE ONE CALLED COMING STORM.

NOPE.

RING
RING
RING

HELLO, WHO IS THIS?

DO YOU REALIZE THAT IT'S SIX O'CLOCK IN THE MORNING?!

NO, THERE'S ONLY AN HOUR DIFFERENCE BETWEEN YOU AND AMHERST.

LUCRATIVE ASSIGNMENT!? WHO IS THIS?

I'M A PARTNER IN AN ANTIQUE BUSINESS BASED HERE IN NEW ORLEANS AND WE NEED A KNOWLEDGEABLE MAN TO DO RESEARCH FOR US.

YOU UNDERSTAND HOW IMPORTANT AUTHENTICATION IS IN MY BUSINESS.

YES. YES, I UNDERSTAND BUT WHY ARE YOU CALLING ME, MR JAMES?

PROFESSOR FITZRANDOLPH, I'VE READ YOUR BOOK ABOUT THE ERA AND YOU HAVE COME HIGHLY RECOMMENDED. I KNOW YOU HAVE A TEACHING POSITION AT THE COLLEGE BUT I WOULD LIKE THE CHANCE TO PERSUADE YOU TO WORK FOR US.

WELL, I - THIS IS A REALLY AWKWARD TIME, MR. JAMES . . . PERHAPS YOU COULD CALL ME AT MY OFFICE LATER TODAY?

I CAN OFFER YOU AN EVEN BETTER ALTERNATIVE, MR. FITZRANDOLPH. I AM CALLING BECAUSE I PLAN TO BE IN NORTHAMPTON ON BUSINESS THIS AFTERNOON AND WOULD LIKE TO MEET YOU FOR DINNER THIS EVENING.

PLEASE EXCUSE THE RUSH BUT I'M LEAVING ON A EUROPEAN BUYING TRIP TOMORROW.

I - UH - I SUPPOSE I COULD MEET YOU BUT, I'LL HAVE TO CONFIRM WITH YOU THIS AFTERNOON. COULD YOU GIVE ME A NUMBER WHERE I CAN REACH YOU?

CHAPIN HALL, AMHERST COLLEGE.
MASSACHUSETTS.
11:15 AM

I HAVE LONG HELD THAT THERE WAS A SOCIETY IN THE LATE 1800'S --

YOU MEAN A "SECRET" SOCIETY, DON'T YOU?

WELL, UM - YES.

AND YOU THINK THAT THEY WERE ABLE TO DEVELOP BABBAGE'S DIFFERENCE ENGINE INTO A WORKING COMPUTER?

I BELIEVE THEY COULD HAVE. THERE IS SOME EVIDENCE AND A CERTAIN CHAIN OF EVENTS THAT HAVE LED ME TO THIS CONCLUSION. BUT I NEED RESEARCHERS TO FIND FACTS TO PROVE IT. SO IF YOU'RE INTERESTED I'LL HAVE A MEETING ON THURSDAY EVENING AFTER CLASS.

NOK-KNOCK!

COME IN.

I WONDERED IF I MIGHT HAVE A MOMENT OF YOUR TIME, FITZRANDOLPH.

I THOUGHT IF WE COULD HAVE A LITTLE INFORMAL CHAT WE MIGHT AVOID AN OFFICIAL MEETING ABOUT SOME CONCERNS THAT I CONTINUE TO HAVE ABOUT YOUR TENURE.

OH. OF COURSE, HAVE A SEAT.

I HEAR THAT YOU ARE INTERVIEWING STUDENTS FOR RESEARCH AGAIN.

WELL, YES I WAS, AND —

EXCUSE ME, BUT IF YOU WILL JUST LET ME FINISH. . . AS I WAS SAYING, IF YOU INTEND TO USE THESE STUDENTS TO ASSIST YOU IN A NEW VENTURE ABOUT YOUR UNSUBSTANTIATED CLAIMS INTO SOME SORT OF VICTORIAN X FILES . . . THEN I SUGGEST YOU RECONSIDER.

YOU HAVEN'T PUBLISHED ANYTHING THAT ACADEMIA WOULD CONSIDER IN OVER A YEAR NOW. IF YOU DON'T PUBLISH, HOW DO YOU EXPECT TO GET TENURE?

I WAS ON A STAKEOUT OF THIS HOOD, GINO SCARPIZZI, THE NEXT DAY. I WAS SPELLING OFF RAY AND STUCK WITH B.S.

SO WE'RE KEEPING AN EYE ON A GREASEBALL CALLED 'N' CHEESE. TELL ME, LEVITICUS, IS THE IRONY OF THIS SITUATION LOST ON YOU OR ARE YOU ABLE TO FULLY APPRECIATE LIFE'S LITTLE JOKES?

LOOK, IF YOU DON'T WANT TO STAY ON THE WIRE TAP THEN JUST TELL ME.

IT'S NOT ANY BIG DEAL, HE'S JUST SHOOTING OFF HIS MOUTH TO HIS STOCK BROKER. TALKING THE SAME CRAP AS HE ALWAYS DOES.

YOU KNOW HOW HE GOT THAT NAME DON'T YOU?

NOPE.

THE FIRST TIME HE WAS LOCKED UP HE WASN'T COVERED BY THE MOB YET. HE WAS AFRAID OF THE CRUISERS IN THE SHOWERS, SO HE DIDN'T SHOWER FOR A MONTH OR SO. I UNDERSTAND HE GOT PRETTY HIGH.

HA HA HAAA! NO SHIT!?

THAT'S WHAT KELLER HEARD.

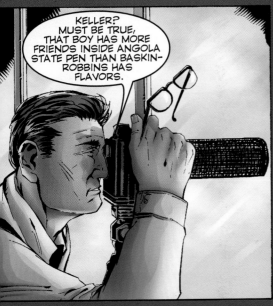

KELLER? MUST BE TRUE, THAT BOY HAS MORE FRIENDS INSIDE ANGOLA STATE PEN THAN BASKIN-ROBBINS HAS FLAVORS.

YOU KNOW KELLER IS A GOOD COP, HARRIMAN. SO WHY DON'T YOU CUT HIM SOME SLACK?

C'MON LEVITICUS, YOU KNOW I'M JUST TALKING. IT DON'T MEAN A THING. IT'S JUST WORD PLAY, M' MAN.

AND IF —

BREE-DEEP!

HEY DOC, KELLER HERE.

SO WHO IS IT?

HAL WANTED ME TO MEET HIM. HE SAID THERE WAS SOMETHING WRONG ABOUT THE SHRINE, BESS. I COULD FEEL AN ICE PICK OF GUILT STAB INTO MY GUT.

IT WAS KELLER, I'VE GOT TO MEET HIM AT THE CORONER'S. LESTER BENOIT IS ON HIS WAY OVER, HE SHOULDN'T BE LONG.

YOU KNOW ME, BESS. I ALWAYS TAKE THE MORAL HIGHROAD. DON'T HELP MYSELF TO ANY CASH LAYING AROUND DRUG BUSTS, WOULD NEVER TAKE A BRIBE.

I'VE ALWAYS BEEN A GOOD COP. BUT I GOT GREEDY AND I MESSED UP A CRIME SCENE. I TAMPERED WITH EVIDENCE, BESS.

DR. LAREN. KELLER. SO, WHAT'S WRONG WITH THE SHRINE?

NOTHING'S WRONG WITH THE SHRINE — WELL, NOT EXACTLY. WHY DON'T I LET ROSE TELL YOU HERSELF, SINCE SHE IS THE ONE WHO FIGURED IT OUT, ANYWAY.

WHEN I SAW THE BONES FROM THE VOODOO SHRINE I KNEW SOMETHING WAS WRONG RIGHT AWAY.

HOW'S THAT?

IF THE BONES HAD BEEN INTERRED THERE WOULD HAVE BEEN STAINING EITHER FROM THE SOIL OR DECOMPOSITION.

AND THEN THERE'S THE EPIPHYSES.

PARDON ME?

THE EPIPHYSES IS THE — UH — CAP OF CARTILAGE AT THE END OF THE BONE. THE DIAPHYSIS IS THE HARD SHAFT OF THE BONE. AS YOU GET OLDER THE TWO GROW TOGETHER. IN WOMEN THE GAP IS GONE BY THE TIME THEY ARE 18 TO 19 YEARS OLD.

ARE YOU TELLING ME THIS IS FROM AN 18 YEAR OLD GIRL?

I AM INDEED.

HOW DO YOU KNOW IT'S A GIRL?

BY THE SIZE THAT IT IS COMPARED TO THE DEVELOPMENT OF THE EPIPHYSES AND THE DIAMETER COMPARED TO THE LENGTH.

THIS CASE JUST KEEPS GETTING BETTER AND BETTER, DON'T IT?

TELL ME ABOUT IT.

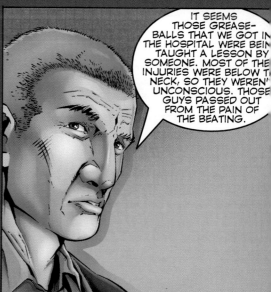

IT SEEMS THOSE GREASE-BALLS THAT WE GOT IN THE HOSPITAL WERE BEIN' TAUGHT A LESSON BY SOMEONE. MOST OF THE INJURIES WERE BELOW T' NECK, SO THEY WEREN'T UNCONSCIOUS. THOSE GUYS PASSED OUT FROM THE PAIN OF THE BEATING.

ARE YOU TRYING TO TELL ME WE GOT A TRAINED KILLER MOUNTING A CAMPAIGN TO REFORM STREET HOODS?

DOC, THERE'S ONLY A HANDFUL OF MEN IN THE WORLD THAT COULD DO WHAT WAS DONE TO THOSE PUNKS. THIS GUY DIDN'T WANT THE ATTENTION OF A TRIPL HOMICIDE BUT HE HAD A REAL NEED TO HURT THOSE BOYS.

HE'S RIGHT, YOU KNOW. FROM WHAT I HEARD FROM THE EMERGENCY WARD THOSE MEN WILL NEED THERAPY TO BE ABLE TO WALK AGAIN. THE AMOUNT OF DAMAGE DONE TO THEM REQUIRED SPECIALIZED KNOWLEDGE OF ANATOMY.

MAYBE SO, BUT I BET THAT HALF THE GUYS TEACHING KARATE IN NEW ORLEANS HAVE THAT SPECIALIZED KNOWLEDGE.

TRUE, BUT WE BETTER GO OVER THE SHRINE AND THE SCENE WITH A FINE TOOTH COMB. HEY, ROSE, IS THERE ANYTHING ELSE YOU CAN TELL US?

NOT UNTIL THE DNA TESTS COME BACK OR YOU FIND ME THE REST OF THE SKELETON.

THEN WE'LL JUST HAVE TO FIND IT, WON'T WE DOC?

IT WAS IN THE FAN NOW. THE ONLY THING I COULD DO WAS TRY TO KEEP TOO MUCH FROM FLYING AROUND.

DOC?

THERE WAS A BOOK, A PAMPHLET. *BEYOND THE WALL OF SLEEP*, THE 1919 EDITION OF LOVECRAFT'S STORY. IT WAS SUCH AN INCREDIBLE FIND THAT I POCKETED IT. I TOOK IT FROM THE CRIME SCENE.

NOW IT'S A MISSING PART OF A PUZZLE. ONE THAT MAY SOLVE THE MURDER OF A YOUNG WOMAN . . . AND I HAVE TO GET IT INTO EVIDENCE EVEN IF IT MARS MY CAREER.

WHEN I THINK OF HOW STUPID IT WAS . . .

AND HOW IT TURNED OUT TO BE FOR NOTHING.

AS WITH SO MANY THINGS . . .

THE BOOK WAS NOT WHAT IT SEEMED.

IT WASN'T EVEN A BOOK.

IT WAS A TRAIN SCHEDULE WRAPPED IN THE COVER O A RARE BOOK.

A VERY OLD TRAIN SCHEDULE . . . THAT SOMEONE HAD DEFACED A PRECIOUS BOOK TO PROTECT.

NOW I KNOW WHAT THE MONKEY WHO GRABBED THE BANANA IN THE JAR FELT LIKE.

UNABLE TO LET GO . . . TRAPPED BY HIS OWN GREED.

NO ONE HAS TRIPPED THE SOSIS WARNING NETS. AND WE HAVEN'T RECEIVED ANY DEMANDS FROM ANY MADMEN. WE STILL CAN'T RULE OUT AN ACCIDENT.

BUT WE HAVE TO BE SURE, GENTLEMEN! WE ARE TALKING ABOUT A BOAT ARMED WITH 16 TRIDENT II MISSILES WITH A PAYLOAD OF 8 - 475 KILOTON YIELD MIRV'S. THESE SLBM'S HAVE A RANGE OF 4600 MILES. THEY DON'T EVEN HAVE TO BE CLOSE TO THE SOSIS! THIS DAMN THING WAS BUILT TO START A WAR!

NONE OF THE DATA SUPPORTS THAT CONCLUSION. IT IS STILL POSSIBLE THAT THE SUB IS BOTTOMED AND IN SOME SORT OF DISTRESS.

THE ADMIRAL IS CORRECT. COLLECTIVELY WE REPRESENT THE RESOURCES OF 16 NATIONS. I SUGGEST WE USE THESE RESOURCES TO LOCATE THIS WEAPON BEFORE SEVERAL BILLION DOLLARS OF BRITISH PROPERTY AND AN UNTOLD COST IN HUMAN LIFE IS LOST FOREVER.

HEAR, HEAR!

WE'VE GOT A LOT OF PEOPLE OUT THERE AND I'M SURE WE WILL FIND SOMETHING. EVEN IF WE HAVE TO DROP ENOUGH SONAR BUOYS TO WALK ACROSS THE OCEAN ON!

NORTH ATLANTIC COUNCIL
DEFENSE PLANNING COMMITTEE
SUPREME HEADQUARTERS ALLIED POWERS
BRUSSELS, BELGIUM

I MISS YOU, BESS. EVERYDAY. AND NIGHT . . . ESPECIALLY WHEN I WAKE UP AT FOUR IN THE MORNING. THE SHEETS TWISTED ACROSS MY CHEST AND YOUR PERFUME STILL HANGING IN THE AIR, LEFT BY A DREAM VISIT THAT IS FADING FROM MY MEMORY LIKE A SUN SHOWER ON LAKE PONTCHARTRAIN.

WELL GIRL, I'D BEST GO GET SOME DINNER ON. I THINK I MIGHT JUST GO AND CATCH THAT FILM FESTIVAL OVER AT TULANE.

BRE-DEET!

BRE-DEET!

NO RESPITE FOR THE WICKED, BESS.

HEY KELLER, WHAT'S UP?

TO BE CONTINUED...

Chapter 5
"The Man Who Cast The Longest Shadow"

I held the book beneath my coat, at pains
To hide the thing from sight in such a place;
...No one had seen me take the thing – but still
A blank laugh echoed in my whirling head.
...I had the book that told the hidden way.

Fungi from Yuggoth
H.P. Lovecraft

NORTHAMPTON, MA.
CENTRE STREET.

EXCUSE ME, I'M SUPPOSED TO MEET A MR. JAMES HERE FOR DINNER?

AH, YES. MR. FITZ-RANDOLPH?

TABLE SIX.

COME WITH ME, SIR.

WINSTON FITZRANDOLPH. PLEASED TO MEET YOU.

SIR.

ANDREW JAMES. IT'S GOOD TO PUT A FACE TO THE NAME, MR. FITZRANDOLPH.

I'LL JUST GIVE YOU A FEW [MI]NUTES WITH THE MENU. PERHAPS YOU WOULD LIKE A DRINK?

NO. NO, [T]HANK YOU. WATER IS FINE.

I'M SURE YOU HAVE MANY QUESTIONS, MR. FITZRANDOLPH. PERHAPS I CAN ANSWER A FEW OF THEM BEFORE WE EAT.

THAT IS TRUE, MR. JAMES, AND I AM CERTAINLY CURIOUS ENOUGH TO HEAR YOU OUT, BUT I THINK I SHOULD WARN YOU THAT I'M LEANING TOWARD NOT ACCEPTING YOUR OFFER. BUT THAT SAID...

MULINO'S

WELL I CAN SEE THE ATTRACTION OF A TENURED POSITION AT AMHERST . . . YOU ARE UP FOR TENURE, ARE YOU NOT? HOWEVER, COMMISSIONED ASSIGNMENTS DO COME WITH NO STRINGS ATTACHED. AS I SAID EARLIER, THEY CAN BE VERY LUCRATIVE.

AND IT WOULD BE MONEY THAT YOU DON'T HAVE TO RUN BY ANY APPROVAL COMMITTEE.

I GET THE FEELING THAT YOU HAVE BEEN CHECKING UP ON ME, MR. JAMES.

NOT AT ALL MR. FITZRANDOLPH. I AM FAMILIAR WITH THE WAY INSTITUTIONS OPERATE AND TO BE HONEST, I DON'T FEEL THAT THEY ARE THE BEST PLACES FOR TRUE SELF-ADVANCEMENT.

WELL I HAVE TO ADMIT THAT THE RED TAPE OF ANY LARGE INSTITUTION CAN BE AGGRAVATING, BUT AMHERST ISN'T QUITE AS TIED UP BY ITS PURSE STRINGS AS MANY SCHOOLS ARE THESE DAYS.

CERTAINLY. AND THE PRESTIGE THAT COMES FROM A POSITION WITH SUCH A SCHOOL DRAWS ATTENTION. IT WAS ONE OF THE THINGS THAT CAUGHT OUR NOTICE WHEN CONSIDERING PROSPECTIVE ASSOCIATES.

BUT I HOPE THAT WASN'T T ONLY THING TH CAUGHT YOUR ATTENTION.

YOU MENTIONED THAT YOU HAD READ MY BOOK 1900.

OH YES! I QUITE ENJOYED IT. ESPECIALLY YOUR ATTENTION TO THE DETAILS OF VICTORIAN LIFE THAT OTHERS SKIM OVER. THE BACK ROOM MACHINATIONS OF POLITICIANS AND THE TITLED - ABSOLUTELY FASCINATING.

WELL IF YOU LIKED THAT YOU'LL LOVE THE ONE I'M WORKING ON NOW. THAT IS, ONCE I GET THROUGH MY RESEARCH.

RESEARCH! NOW THAT IS REALLY WHY I AM TALKING TO YOU. WE HAD NEVER SEEN SUCH THOROUGH RESEARCH ON A TOPIC. THE INDEXES AND BIBLIOGRAPHY ALONE WERE WORTH THE PRICE OF THE BOOK.

BUT I MUST ADMIT MY KNOWLEDGE IS VERY RESTRICTED TO THAT PERIOD AND I WOULD THINK THAT YOUR COMPANY WOULD WANT AN ART HISTORIAN OR AT LEAST SOMEONE WITH A MORE THOROUGH KNOWLEDGE.

NO, NO, NO. BECAUSE OF THE VENTURE WE ARE ENTERING INTO WITH A BRITISH COLLECTOR WE REQUIRE A VERY SPECIFIC KNOWLEDGE OF THINGS VICTORIAN. AND A LOT OF THE GOODS WE ARE LOOKING AT ARE NEITHER FURNITURE NOR PAINTINGS.

ARE WE READY?

WHA?

PARDON ME SIR. I JUST WONDERED IF YOU WERE READY TO ORDER.

"DON'T YOU JUST LOVE THOSE LONG RAINY AFTERNOONS IN NEW ORLEANS WHEN AN HOUR ISN'T JUST AN HOUR - BUT A LITTLE PIECE OF ETERNITY DROPPED INTO YOUR HANDS - AND WHO KNOWS WHAT TO DO WITH IT?" - *A STREETCAR NAMED DESIRE*, TENNESSEE WILLIAMS.

1313 CHARTRES, THE FRENCH QUARTER.

BABINEAUX!

WE'D LIKE TO HAVE A WORD WITH YOU TRASCLAIR.

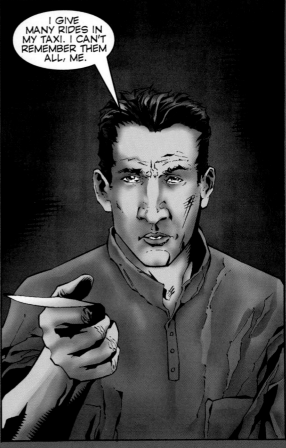

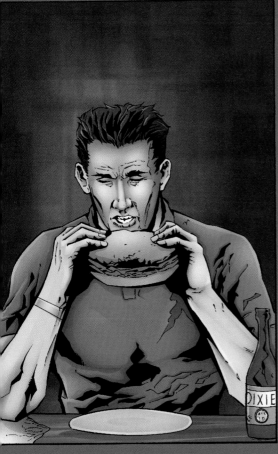

I REMEMBER THE NIGHT ...

MAKE LIKE DAT FO'... CRAZY OL' CABRI!

LET'S GO.

WHERE'S DAT YOU WON' GO?

JUST DRIVE!

PLEASE.

LISTEN, T-GIRL . . . YOU BES' GIVE ME YO' DESTINATION.

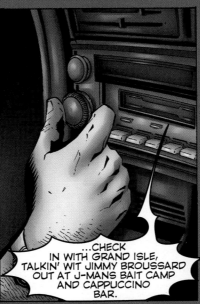

...CHECK IN WITH GRAND ISLE, TALKIN' WIT JIMMY BROUSSARD OUT AT J-MANS BAIT CAMP AND CAPPUCCINO BAR.

JIMMY, HOW THEY BITIN' DIS WEEK?

REAL SLOW SO FAR --

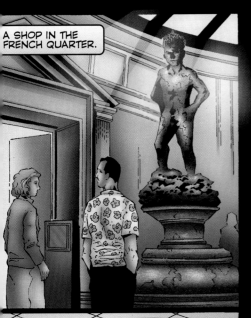

A SHOP IN THE FRENCH QUARTER.

NORTHAMPTON, MASSACHUSETTS

"NO, THANK YOU, I HAVE A LIFE HERE AND I'M NOT INTERESTED IN LEAVING." THAT'S WHAT I SAID, BUT NOW THE WORDS RING HOLLOW.

IT SAYS THAT THIS IS THE VOODOO SPIRIT, EXU. THE FOUNTAIN IS HERE TO RECEIVE OFFERINGS. IT SAYS THAT HE LIKES SHINY THINGS ...

EXU

I GUESS THE DEAN'S RAMBLINGS HAVE GOT ME MORE SHOOK UP THAN I THOUGHT. WELL, I WON'T HAVE TO WORRY ABOUT THAT ONCE MY TENURE HAS BEEN GRANTED.

WHAT IS IT?

WHY, I GUESS IT'S A WISHING WELL. IT SAYS HE IS THE TRICKSTER SPIRIT AND OFFERINGS BRING GOOD LUCK.

WOULD HAVE NEVER LET HIM WORRY ME WHEN NATALIE AND I WERE STILL TOGETHER.

THE FRENCH QUARTER, URSULINES.

REMEMBERING...

TRASCLAIR?

A GALLERY OPENING ON DUMAINE.

TITUS GETS THE GUN BECAUSE HE'S A GOOD SHOT. AND ANYWAY, LAST TIME YOU HAD IT YOU NEARLY SHOT ME! NOW YOU GO AND KEEP AN EYE OUT FOR THE MAN, WE GOTTA DO!

FINE!

MAN, I DON'T KNOW WHAT YOU SEE IN THAT BITCH.

DIS AN' DAT, MON. DIS AN' DAT.

C'MON DEAR, MAKE A WISH.

NOW WHAT KIND OF FINANCIER WOULD I BE, TOSSING MONEY IN THAT THING?

I KNOW THAT PROMOTION IS A BIG ONE . . . BUT CAN'T YOU PUT ASIDE WORK TILL OUR VACATION IS OVER?

SORRY HONEY, BUT, WELL I GUESS I'LL ALWAYS BE SERIOUS ABOUT MONEY.

NATALIE COULD NEVER COME TO TERMS WITH MY VISION. SHE . . . I SHOULDN'T TALK IN ABSOLUTES. IT WASN'T THE VISION, IT WAS THE LACK OF RECOGNITION. MY FAILURE TO PURSUE ANOTHER AVENUE TO SUCCESS.

OBSESSION. IT ISN'T OBSESSION IF YOU HAPPEN TO BE RIGHT. WHEN DID MY CONFIDENCE BECOME A NEUROSIS, NATALIE? WHEN DID FOCUS GIVE BIRTH TO OBSESSION?

birth?

YOU GOTTA BLOW THE GUY'S HEAD OFF, MAN . . . HE WALKS AWAY FROM THIS, WE DON'T GET THE REST OF THE PAYOUT AN' YOU KNOW THAT'S THE JACKPOT, MAN.

IT'S DE SHIT, MAN. WE BE SET FOR LIFE.

HEY! CAB DRIVER, YOU GOT SOMETHIN' THAT BELONGS TO ME!

AN' ALL THAT'S BETWEEN US AN' TH' MONEY IS SOME GEEK.

SOOO ... WHAT COLOR MERCEDES YOU SAY YOU LAK?

I'VE BEEN FEELING SORRY FOR MYSELF AND THINKING NATALIE LEFT BECAUSE I WAS SUCH A FAILURE BUT . . BUT --

WAS IT HER BIOLOGICAL CLOCK WINDING DOWN? AND WHAT KIND OF FATHER WOULD SHE THINK I'D MAKE? IS THAT WHY SHE NEEDED SOME TIME ON HER OWN?

NO. IT ISN'T THAT SIMPLE. IF IT WAS, SHE WOULD HAVE TOLD ME, NATALIE IS NO SHRINKING VIOLET ... AND YOU DON'T JUST THROW AWAY NINE YEARS OF YOUR LIFE.

AN' YOU, T-GIRL. DER'S DE MATTER OF DE FARE YOU OWE OL' TRACE, ME.

IT'S NONE OF THOSE THINGS AND IT'S ALL OF THOSE THINGS. IT'S HER NEEDS AND WANTS STACKED UP AGAINST MINE, AND OUR RELATIONSHIP WAS WHERE THOSE NEEDS AND WANTS REFLECTED EACH OTHER.

THERE IS NO SIMPLE ANSWER. IF I WAS AN ALCOHOLIC OR AN UNREPENTANT GAMBLER OR WIFE BEATER, THEN IT WOULD BE OBVIOUS. BUT NATALIE AND I ALWAYS GOT ALONG. WE MAY HAVE ARGUED BUT WE DIDN'T FIGHT.

SHE JUST NEEDED SOME PERSPECTIVE. AND I, I NEED TO SHOW HER THAT I CAN MAKE IT WORK. THINGS WILL BE DIFFERENT ONCE I HEAR FROM THE BOARD ABOUT MY APPLICATION FOR TENURE.

GET YOU NEST BUILT GIRL. I AIN'T BOUT TO HURT YOU, NO. FACT, DE T-GIRL DAT HUNT ME DOWN ON MY DAY OFF DESERVE T' GET HER SHAWS WITHOUT PAYIN' DE FARE.

DON'T DO ME ANY FAVORS. I'VE GOT YOUR TWO DOLLARS AND NINETY CENTS RIGHT HERE.

JUS' BE COOL, WOMAN. WE GOTS PLENNY O' TIME. HEY, DUDE?

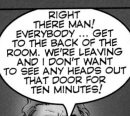

RIGHT THERE MAN! EVERYBODY ... GET TO THE BACK OF THE ROOM. WE'RE LEAVING AND I DON'T WANT TO SEE ANY HEADS OUT THAT DOOR FOR TEN MINUTES!

... he's in a bright yellow flower print shirt, just up the street.

YEEEHAA!

OUT A' DE WAY, MAN! OUT A' DE WAY!!

OOOF!

OH, DEAR GOD!

C'MON MAN! COME! ON!

TO BE CONTINUED...

Chapter 6

Fin De Siècle

Behold the image of my fear.
O rise not, move not, come not near!
That moment, when you turned your face,
 A demon seemed to leap through space;
 His gesture strangled me with fear.

Haschisch
Arthur Symons

IN EVERY LARGE CITY THERE ARE THOUSANDS LIKE THESE, FOOTPADS AND SHOPLIFTERS; PIMPS AND WHORES' BULLIES; BUG-HUNTERS AND SNOOZERS AND ALL THOSE OTHER CRIMINAL TYPES WHO LIVE BY PLUNDER, CHEATING AND WHEN OCCASION DEMANDS, BY VIOLENCE.

NO DOUBT RAISED IN SOME ROOKERY WHERE CRIME AND MISERY JOSTLED EACH OTHER, WHERE ANY LATENT DISPOSITION TO DEPRAVITY AND VICE WOULD SURELY BE FOSTERED AND DEVELOPED.

YOU'D ALSO KNOW THAT THE LOWER LEVEL DOORS ARE LOCKED TO DISCOURAGE THE HOMELESS FROM TAKING UP RESIDENCE IN THE STAIRS.

MOLEEEEEN!! YOU BASTAAARD!!!

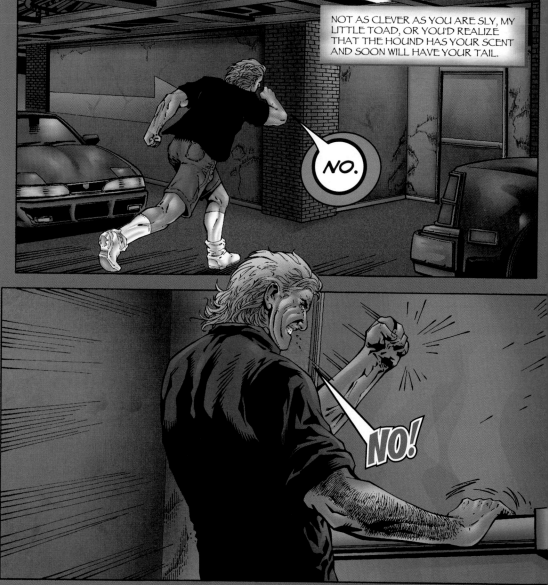

NOT AS CLEVER AS YOU ARE SLY, MY LITTLE TOAD, OR YOU'D REALIZE THAT THE HOUND HAS YOUR SCENT AND SOON WILL HAVE YOUR TAIL.

NO.

NO!

I HEAR Y' BARON ... I HEAR YOU BUT I AIN'T GON' BE YOUR RIDE! NO! NOT DIS BOY.

YYOOOOOO ARRRE GOIIIIINN TOOOO SUUU'UFFFAAAAA ASSS THOSSSSSSS WAHHOOOOO SUU'FFFAAAAA'D AITT YO AAAAANDS!!!

THOU ART DEATH'S FOOL; FOR HIM THOU LABOUR'ST BY THY FLIGHT TO SHUN, AND YET RUN'ST TOWARD HIM.

PITY.

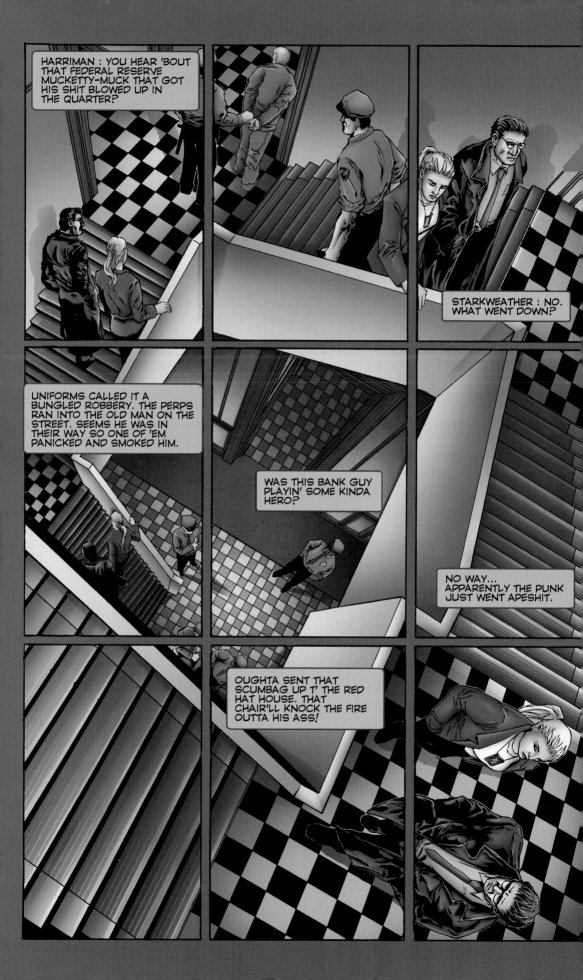

WHO YOU GIVING THE DEATH PENALTY NOW RAY?

AHH ... JUS' SOME LOWLIFE THAT KILLED THAT OLD BANKER COUPL'A HOURS AGO. YOU HEARD, HUH?

I HAVEN'T HEARD ANYTHING. I SWEAR THAT I'VE BEEN ON THIS SCARPIZZI THING SO LONG THAT MY BRAIN IS NUMB.

WORKING WITH THOSE TREASURY STIFFS WILL DO THAT TO YOU.

SO WHY IS THE MOB DEALING CARDS OUT TO A LOSER LIKE VINNIE ANY WAY?

I MEAN, DON'T THEY JUST SMUGGLE THEIR CASH OUT OF THE COUNTRY IN MILLION DOLLAR BALES?

VINNIE IS GIFTED.

YEAH! GIFTED LIKE THE JANITOR'S RETARD KID! HAH!

OH MAN, BS.

WHAT?

AS I WAS SAYING ... SCARPIZZI SEEMS TO BE A VERY GOOD ACCOUNTANT.

GET OUTTA' HERE!

NO SHIT! THE TREASURY BULLS CAN'T FIND A PAPER TRAIL. HE'S GOT SO MANY LAYERS OF COMPLEX FINANCIAL TRANSACTIONS THAT THEIR HEADS ARE SPINNING. AND THE KICKER IS IT ALL SPELLS OUT AS LEGIT!

I DON'T BELIEVE IT.

BELIEVE IT. WHY DO YOU THINK WE'RE RUNNING THIS STAKEOUT?

C'MON! THE CHEESE THINKS ADDITION IS AN EXTRA ROOM ON HIS HOUSE, NEVERMIND COOKING BOOKS LIKE A PRO!

IF YOU'RE HAVIN' TROUBLE WITH THAT CONCEPT, B.S., YOU'LL NEVER HANDLE WHAT OWENS BROUGHT IN TODAY.

OH YEAH. TRY ME.

OWENS IS OUT ON HIS BEAT WHEN THIS GUY STUMBLES UP AND TURNS HIMSELF IN FOR THOSE KARAOKE BAR ROBBERIES.

ANOTHER FRIGGIN' PENITENT!

THAT'S THE FOURTH ONE THIS MONTH. WHAT THE HELL IS GOIN' ON?

THEY ALL MUMBLED SOME JUNK ABOUT "THE HAT," WHATEVER THAT MEANS, BUT WE HAVEN'T GOT ANY OTHER LEADS.

SOUNDS LIKE SOME VOODOO SHIT, DOC. IS THAT WHY THE CHIEF HAS YOU AND G.I. JOE ON THE CASE?

LAUGH IT UP, FAT BOY.

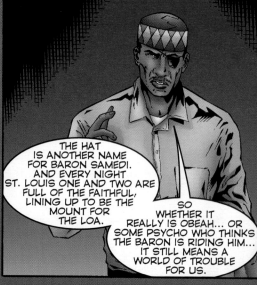

THE HAT IS ANOTHER NAME FOR BARON SAMEDI. AND EVERY NIGHT ST. LOUIS ONE AND TWO ARE FULL OF THE FAITHFUL, LINING UP TO BE THE MOUNT FOR THE LOA.

SO WHETHER IT REALLY IS OBEAH... OR SOME PSYCHO WHO THINKS THE BARON IS RIDING HIM... IT STILL MEANS A WORLD OF TROUBLE FOR US.

AS THE VICTORIAN ERA RACED TOWARD THE END OF THE CENTURY, UNPARALLELED ECONOMIC, SCIENTIFIC, POLITICAL AND INTELLECTUAL CHANGES WERE TAKING PLACE UNLIKE ANYTHING EXPERIENCED BEFORE IN BRITISH HISTORY.

SOCIETY ATTEMPTED TO RESTORE ITS EQUILIBRIUM BY SEEKING UNCHANGEABLE ABSOLUTES. OF COURSE, THIS PRECIPITATED A MULTITUDE OF DIVERSE VOICES CRYING OUT TO HAVE "THEIR" TRUTH RECOGNIZED.

JUST AS TODAY, WITH OUR ENTRY INTO THE NEW MILLENNIUM, THE 1890s EXPERIENCED FRUSTRATION AND CONFUSION BROUGHT ABOUT BY PROGRESSIVE CHANGE.

AND, SIMILAR TO OUR TIME, MANY PLACED THEIR HOPES FOR THE FUTURE IN THE TECHNOLOGY THAT SURROUNDED THEM.

SOME TURNED TO NATURE AS THE ONLY TRUE CONSTANT IN LIFE AND TOOK COMFORT IN ITS INEVITABLE RENEWAL.

THERE WAS ALSO THE SCHOOL OF THOUGHT THAT BELIEVED NO ANSWERS EXISTED OUTSIDE OF ONE'S OWN SELF AND THAT IT WAS A MISTAKE TO SEEK EXTERNAL CERTAINTY.

A FIN DE SIÈCLE WRITER NAMED ARTHUR SYMONS EXPRESSED SELF RELIANCE IN HIS POEM, HASCHISCH:

AND YET I AM THE LORD OF ALL,
AND THIS BRAVE WORLD MAGNIFICAL,
VEILED IN SO VARIABLE A MIST
IT MAY BE ROSE OR AMETHYST,
DEMANDS ME FOR THE LORD OF ALL!

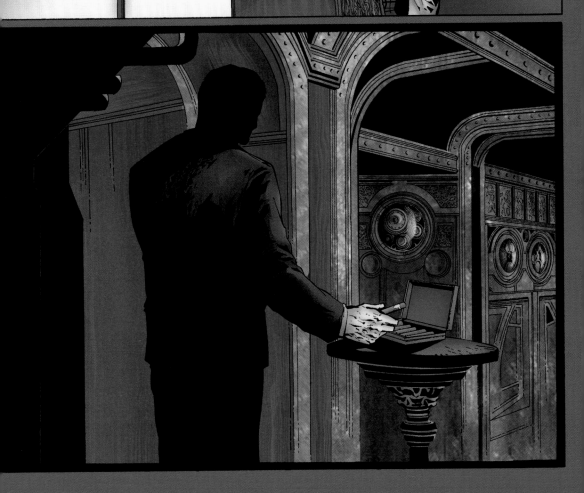

WITH THE BELIEF THAT HUMAN LIFE WAS FLEETING AND DIFFICULT TO UNDERSTAND, LIVELY INTELLECTUAL DISCOURSE BEGAN TO FIND A HOME IN THE SECRET SOCIETIES AND CLUBS THAT ORGANIZED IN THE SEARCH FOR ENLIGHTENMENT.

Romanticism: Early 1800s – Byron, Shelley, Kea
Realism: 1830s + 40s – Dickens, Trollope, Bolza
Naturalism: Grew out of Realism, Wharton, Zo
Decadence and Aestheticism: 1870s, 80s + 90s –
Wilde, Carlyle, Yeats – 'art for art's se

IT IS MY OPINION, BASED ON EXHAUSTIVE RESEARCH, THAT ONE OR TWO OF THESE SOCIETIES MAY HAVE REDIRECTED OUR FUTURE IN WAYS THAT WE AREN'T EVEN AWARE OF TODAY.

MANY OF YOU KNOW THAT, I HAVE PUBLISHED ESSAYS ON THE FIN DE SIÈCLE WHICH ADDRESS THE THEORETICAL POSSIBILITY OF AN ELITE INTELLECTUAL CADRE CAPABLE OF UNPARALLELED ACHIEVEMENT AND WHOSE HIDDEN OR DISGUISED ACCOMPLISHMENTS ARE DIRECTLY AFFECTING OUR CURRENT WORLD.

AMHERST

Professor FitzRandolph;

We regret to inform you that at this time the board cannot approve your request for tenure. Upon consideration of your performance as a representative of this learning centre and your continued insubordination concerning the wishes of the board, we intend to cease offering the course that has been solely taught by you.

"The Victorian Age: Fin de Siècle" will see its final session with the close of this semester. We would glad... recommendati... an assistant... ...sit...

I BELIEVE THAT I AM CLOSE TO VERIFYING THE EXISTENCE OF SUCH A GROUP AND I AM LEAVING AMHERST TO DEVOTE MY FULL ATTENTION TO THIS EFFORT.

YOU DID WHAT!

I'M THE GUY THAT WUZ CREEPIN' THOSE 'PARTMENTS IN THE QUARTER. I - UH - WELL I THINK IT WUZ 'RONG AN' I COME HERE TO TURN MYSELF IN, SIR.

I - I PAWNED THE STUFF SO I DON'T GOT IT NO MORE BUT I MADE A LIST A' THE PAWN SHOPS I USED.

OH YEAH...

WELL, YOU BETTER TAKE A SEAT OVER THERE 'TIL I CAN GET SOMEONE TO TAKE YOUR STATEMENT.

OO - OVER THERE?

I'D REALLY 'PRECIATE YOU GETTIN' SOMEBODY REAL SOON 'CAUSE "THE HAT" WANTS ME TO DO THIS RIGHT AN' I DON' WANT HIM GETTIN' PISSED AGIN. OKAY?

YOU BETTER GIT YOUR ASS OVER TO THAT SEAT OR YOU'LL HAVE MORE TO WORRY ABOUT THAN JUST THE HAT, Y'HEAR?!

HEY, INGRAM. LET ONE OF THE DETECTIVES KNOW WE GOT ANOTHER ONE OF THOSE 'PENITENTS'.

ELSEWHERE ON THE STREETS OF NEW ORLEANS.

DIN' MEAN NO HARM...

JUS' WANT WHUT'S IN YO' GROCERY TILL...

PLEASE DON' BE GOIN' FO' NO GUN MR. CHINAMAN

OH M' CLAUDETTE... YOU SHOULDN' OUGHTA SLEP WIT SONNY BOY, GIRL.

DON' BE PUSHIN' ME WHEN I GOTS A KNIFE, CLAUDETTE.

BON DIEU, GIRL... YOU GOT - SO - MUCH - BLOOD.

so much blood...

so much blood...

so much blood on my hands.

NEW ORLEANS, GARDEN DISTRICT
PRYTANIA STREET
THE HOME OF CLAUDE BALLARÉ.

THE WAR HEADS?

CONSIDER THEM HANDLED, MR. BALLARÉ.

AND WHAT OF THE CREW?

ABSOLUTELY, SIR. EXCUSE MY INFORMALITY.

QUITE ALRIGHT, MR. CROWN. I'M SURE THAT WE ALL ARE AWARE OF THE GRAVITY OF THE ENTERPRISE THAT WE ARE EMBARKING ON TODAY.

THE FUTURE EVOLUTION OF THE HUMAN RACE DEPENDS ON THE SUCCESS OF OUR EFFORTS, MR. CROWN.

THAT ASIDE, LET ME BE THE FIRST TO CONGRATULATE YOU BOTH ON THE SUCCESSFUL COMPLETION OF THE FIRST STAGE OF OUR OPERATION.

SIR.

BUT RATHER THAN TOAST OUR EFFORTS IN THE PAST, MR. CROWN, MS. WHITE, I THINK IT MUCH MORE APPROPRIATE THAT WE LOOK TO THE FUTURE.

TO THE FUTURE!

TO BE CONTINUED...

Societas Clandestina Aeterna [Eternal Cabal]
by Tim Bradstreet and Grant Goleash

WELL
I'LL BE GOD-
DAMNED.

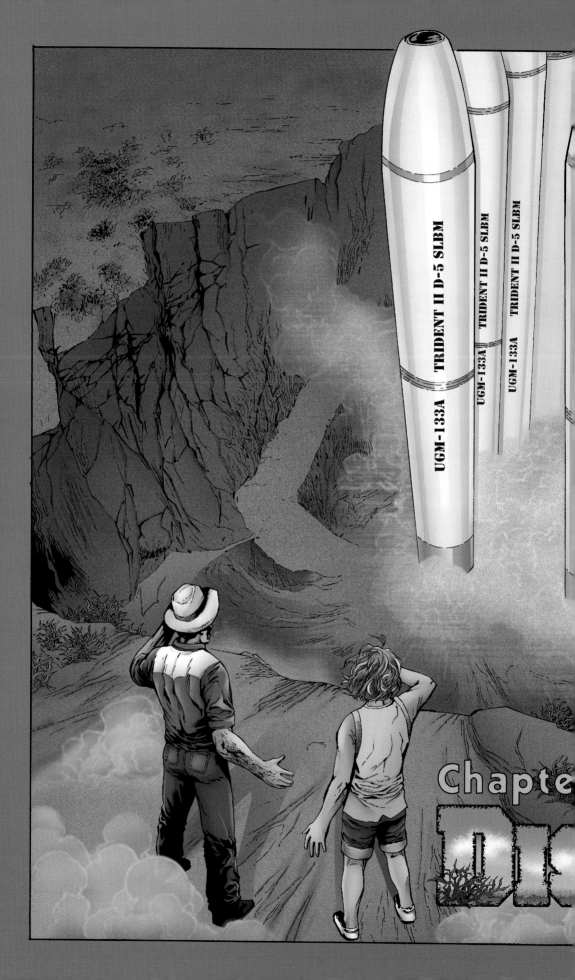

UGM-133A TRIDENT II D-5 SLBM

UGM-133A TRIDENT II D-5 SLBM

UGM-133A TRIDENT II D-5 SLBM

UGM-133A TRIDENT II D-5 SLBM

Now is not the end. It is not even the beginning of
the end. But is, perhaps, the end of the beginning...
Winston Churchill
Nov. 10, 1942
Speech at the Mansion House, London

INTERMENT

Egham, England
College of the Order
Of the Blue Rose
Fall of 1885

Dear Olasha,
  England is a very rainy place, but I have a wonderful room here at the Order's school. You would like it a lot. Mr. Gosney showed me a picture of the new house that he bought for you and Mama and Papa. Now I know that you have your own room to put the dollhouse that I got you before I left.

Mr. Gosney left me at the school yesterday. He introduced me to a Mr. Davidson who will be one of my teachers. We are the only people here right now besides the servants. Mr. Davidson said that there are eleven other children enrolled here and they will be arriving next week.

Mr. Davidson showed me around the school yesterday. The building used to be the manor house of a large estate. There are over one hundred rooms. I hope you can come to visit sometime. There is a stable and horses for everyone, that means one for you if you come.

New Orleans, 1999

NOK-
NK-
NK

WHO D'FUK'A YOU?

NAME'S TITUS. ME AN MY CREW DONE A JOB FOR SONNY DEE. HE SAID ANYTHIN' GOES WRONG WE SHOULD COME HERE.

WHOA!

WHO'S AT?

D'KNOW, SEZ SONNY TOL' HIM HE SHOULD GO HERE IF HE'S INNA SHITTER.

SO ASK 'IM HIS NAME, VITO.

HEY PAL, WHATCHER NAME?

HEY? DREAMBOY!

'S TITUS...

HEY, PALLY, YOU HEAR ME, HUH?

Dear Olasha,
Today the rest of the students attending the school arrived. It was a beautiful day and we had a lot of fun helping them get settled in their rooms.

After everyone had been properly installed in their rooms, we all met in the salon for high tea. You would have loved it, Lasha. There were crumpets, cucumber sandwiches, clotted cream and strawberries, macaroons and your favorite - meringues.

A great time was had by all and we were all eager to make new friends.

Well, almost everyone.
I met this French girl, Lily and she was incredibly rude and snobbish. She doesn' make it very easy for anyone to like her.

When we were finished with tea, the butler came in and directed us to the library. I had been talking to a boy named Ghulam Mohammed. He is from a town called Amritsar in India.

I think he and I shall be the best of friends.

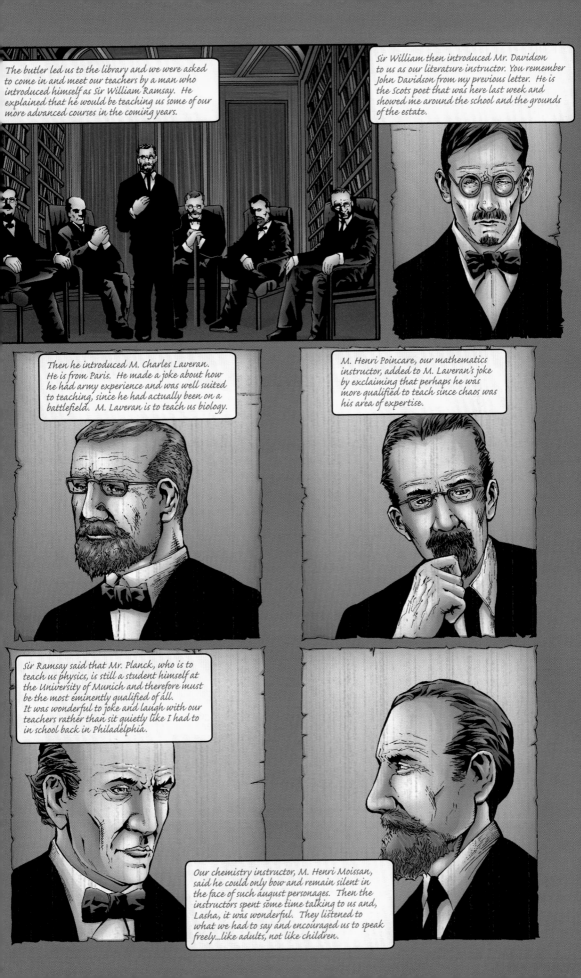

The butler led us to the library and we were asked to come in and meet our teachers by a man who introduced himself as Sir William Ramsay. He explained that he would be teaching us some of our more advanced courses in the coming years.

Sir William then introduced Mr. Davidson to us as our literature instructor. You remember John Davidson from my previous letter. He is the Scots poet that was here last week and showed me around the school and the grounds of the estate.

Then he introduced M. Charles Laveran. He is from Paris. He made a joke about how he had army experience and was well suited to teaching, since he had actually been on a battlefield. M. Laveran is to teach us biology.

M. Henri Poincaré, our mathematics instructor, added to M. Laveran's joke by exclaiming that perhaps he was more qualified to teach since chaos was his area of expertise.

Sir Ramsay said that Mr. Planck, who is to teach us physics, is still a student himself at the University of Munich and therefore must be the most eminently qualified of all. It was wonderful to joke and laugh with our teachers rather than sit quietly like I had to in school back in Philadelphia.

Our chemistry instructor, M. Henri Moissan, said he could only bow and remain silent in the face of such august personages. Then the instructors spent some time talking to us and, Lasha, it was wonderful. They listened to what we had to say and encouraged us to speak freely...like adults, not like children.

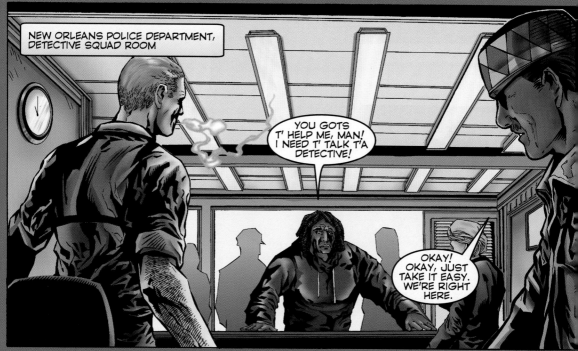

NEW ORLEANS POLICE DEPARTMENT, DETECTIVE SQUAD ROOM

YOU GOTS T' HELP ME, MAN! I NEED T' TALK T'A DETECTIVE!

OKAY! OKAY, JUST TAKE IT EASY. WE'RE RIGHT HERE.

I GOT DE GRIS-GRIS ON ME SOMPIN' BAD. I GOTS T' CONFESS OR DE HAT HE COME FOR ME!

THE HAT? DO YOU MEAN THE BARON SAMEDI?

NOW TELL US ABOUT THIS HAT DUDE...JUST WHAT'S HE LOOK LIKE?

HE'S TALL AND DARK, WEARIN' A SHINY BLACK TOP HAT. HIS EYES, DEY BIG AND GLITTER LIKE DARK EMERALDS. HE COME IN ON CLOUDS A' HIS TOBACCO SMOKE - HE WANTS ME TO TELL YOU HOW I KILLED DE MAN.

NOW I'VE SEEN IT ALL! I'M NOT BUYING ANY OF THIS VOODOO CRAP! YOU TELL ME YOU KILLED A MAN BUT YOU'RE INNOCENT 'CAUSE THE CAT IN THE HAT TOLD YOU TO DO IT!

KELLER! JUST BACK OFF AND GIVE THE MAN SOME ROOM TO SPEAK.

De Hat a monter l'cheval, he...oh m' gros bon ange.

NOW YOU TELL ME, DID YOU HEAR THE LOA TELL YOU TO KILL A MAN?

DE GUÉDÉS DON' TELL TO KILL. DE HAT HE MAKES ME CONFESS MY SINS. HE MADE ME HIS SERVITEUR AN' I GOT TO CONFESS OR HE GIVE MY POT-DE-TETE TO HIS GRANDE BRIGITTE.

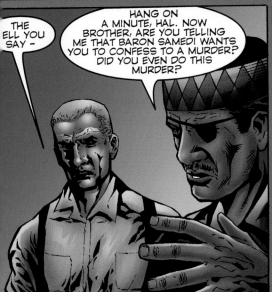

THE ELL YOU SAY –

HANG ON A MINUTE, HAL. NOW BROTHER, ARE YOU TELLING ME THAT BARON SAMEDI WANTS YOU TO CONFESS TO A MURDER? DID YOU EVEN DO THIS MURDER?

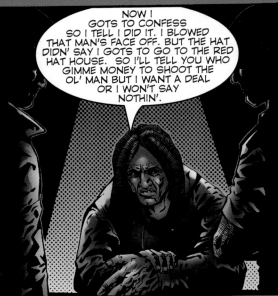

NOW I GOTS TO CONFESS SO I TELL I DID IT. I BLOWED THAT MAN'S FACE OFF. BUT THE HAT DIDN' SAY I GOTS TO GO TO THE RED HAT HOUSE. SO I'LL TELL YOU WHO GIMME MONEY TO SHOOT THE OL' MAN BUT I WANT A DEAL OR I WON'T SAY NOTHIN'.

HOLD UP NOW BROTHER... ARE YOU SAYING THAT THE MAN SHOT IN THE QUARTER WAS A HIT?

I AIN' EVEN GIVIN' YOU DE GREASEBALL'S FAVRIT COLOR 'LESS YOU START TELLIN' ME WHAT KINDA DEAL I KIN 'SPECT.

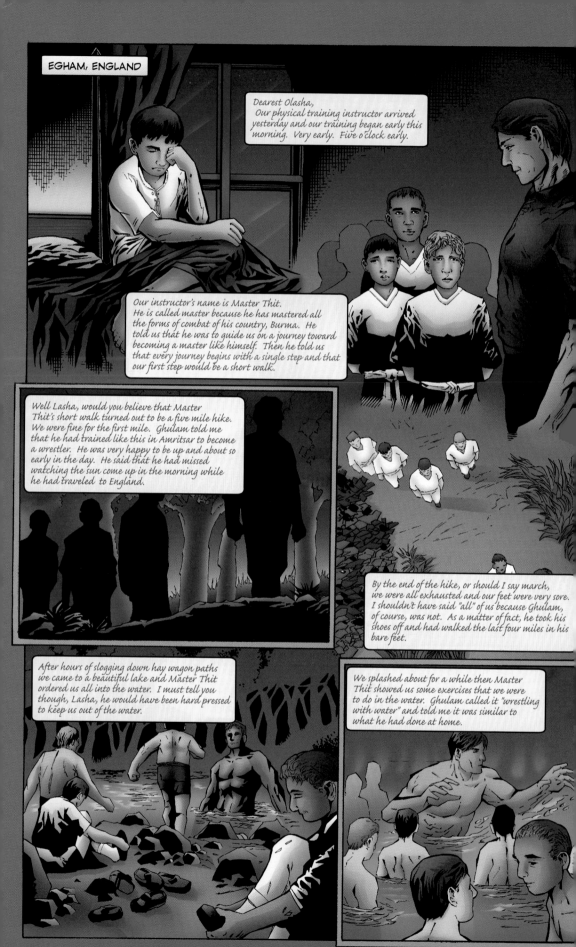

EGHAM, ENGLAND

Dearest Olasha,
Our physical training instructor arrived yesterday and our training began early this morning. Very early. Five o'clock early.

Our instructor's name is Master Thit. He is called master because he has mastered all the forms of combat of his country, Burma. He told us that he was to guide us on a journey toward becoming a master like himself. Then he told us that every journey begins with a single step and that our first step would be a short walk.

Well Lasha, would you believe that Master Thit's short walk turned out to be a five mile hike. We were fine for the first mile. Ghulam told me that he had trained like this in Amritsar to become a wrestler. He was very happy to be up and about so early in the day. He said that he had missed watching the sun come up in the morning while he had traveled to England.

By the end of the hike, or should I say march, we were all exhausted and our feet were very sore. I shouldn't have said "all" of us because Ghulam, of course, was not. As a matter of fact, he took his shoes off and had walked the last four miles in his bare feet.

After hours of slogging down hay wagon paths we came to a beautiful lake and Master Thit ordered us all into the water. I must tell you though, Lasha, he would have been hard pressed to keep us out of the water.

We splashed about for a while then Master Thit showed us some exercises that we were to do in the water. Ghulam called it "wrestling with water" and told me it was similar to what he had done at home.

After we had finished our swimming exercises,
Master Thit had us stand in rows and began to
teach us the Lai Ka, which means the Fight Dance.
He said he would bring a drum next time so we
may follow its rhythm when we dance tomorrow.

Master Thit laughed at our reaction to
his news about tomorrow, then he told us
that by the winter we would be running
the five miles that we had hiked. And
that we would even look forward to it.

Lasha, if anyone else had told me that, I might
have snapped back some sort of smart alec retort.
But Master Thit seems to have such confidence
in us that I couldn't imagine ever treating him
with anything but respect.

We took a short rest and drank some water
from an Artesian well that was nearby and
then we started the hike back to the school.
And mercifully, a short nap before our
morning classes began.

Dearest Olasha,
   There are so many things to learn here about everything. There are times when I really miss the simplicity of my life before the College of the Order of the Blue Rose.

Mr. Wooster, our butler, spent an entire evening teaching us the proper way to sit down to dine. I don't mean he took all that time to show us how to sit in a chair, that was only part of the lesson.

Mr. Wooster stopped us at each step of the way and lectured us on the significance of our actions.

Lasha, when Mr. Gosney brought me across the ocean on the ship he showed me how to use a napkin, but the fancy folded linen at our table in the college didn't look like anything I'd expected.

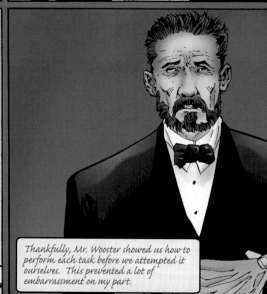

Thankfully, Mr. Wooster showed us how to perform each task before we attempted it ourselves. This prevented a lot of embarrassment on my part.

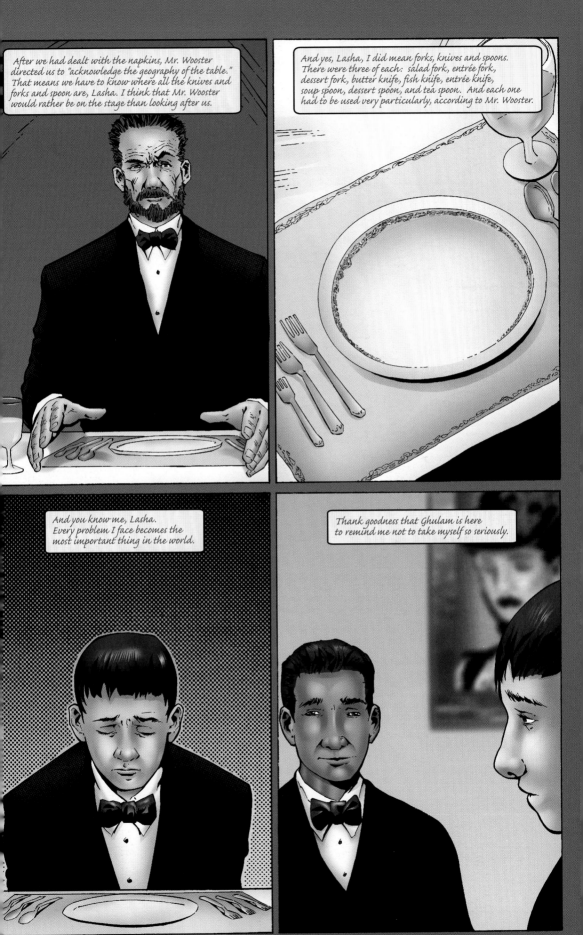

After we had dealt with the napkins, Mr. Wooster directed us to "acknowledge the geography of the table." That means we have to know where all the knives and forks and spoon are, Lasha. I think that Mr. Wooster would rather be on the stage than looking after us.

And yes, Lasha, I did mean forks, knives and spoons. There were three of each: salad fork, entrée fork, dessert fork, butter knife, fish knife, entrée knife, soup spoon, dessert spoon, and tea spoon. And each one had to be used very particularly, according to Mr. Wooster.

And you know me, Lasha. Every problem I face becomes the most important thing in the world.

Thank goodness that Ghulam is here to remind me not to take myself so seriously.

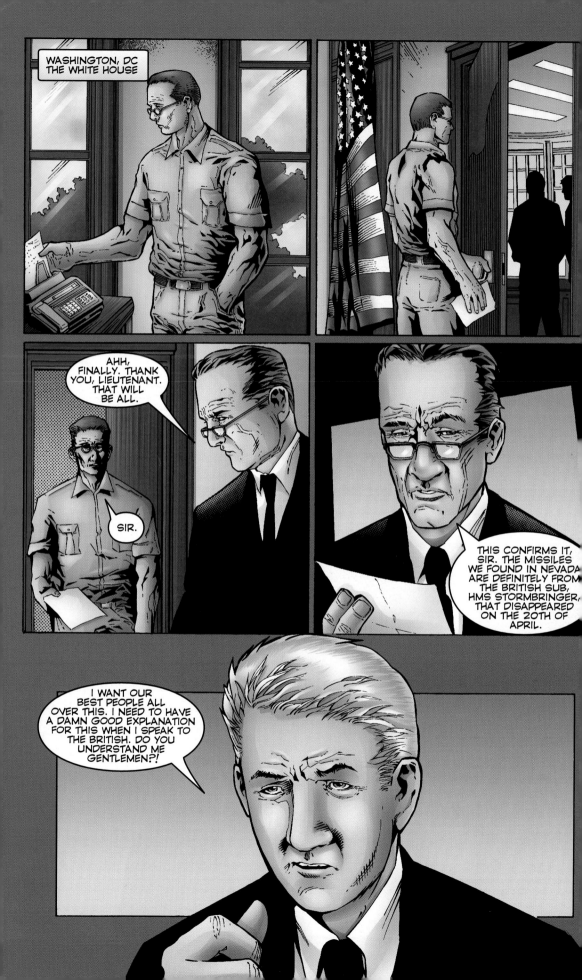

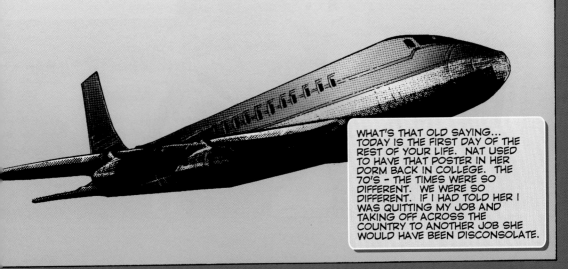

30,000 FEET BOUND FOR NEW ORLEANS.

WHAT'S THAT OLD SAYING... TODAY IS THE FIRST DAY OF THE REST OF YOUR LIFE. NAT USED TO HAVE THAT POSTER IN HER DORM BACK IN COLLEGE. THE 70'S – THE TIMES WERE SO DIFFERENT. WE WERE SO DIFFERENT. IF I HAD TOLD HER I WAS QUITTING MY JOB AND TAKING OFF ACROSS THE COUNTRY TO ANOTHER JOB SHE WOULD HAVE BEEN DISCONSOLATE.

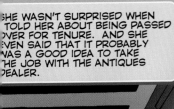

SHE WASN'T SURPRISED WHEN I TOLD HER ABOUT BEING PASSED OVER FOR TENURE. AND SHE EVEN SAID THAT IT PROBABLY WAS A GOOD IDEA TO TAKE THE JOB WITH THE ANTIQUES DEALER.

THAT I SHOULD USE THIS OPPORTUNITY TO FINANCE THE RESEARCH ON MY BOOK. WHAT SHE REALLY MEANT WAS THAT I SHOULD TAKE THE MONEY AND EXORCISE MY GHOSTS. THAT I WON'T BE ABLE TO PURSUE A PROFESSORSHIP UNTIL I DO.

I HOPE TO GOD THAT SHE CAN WAIT FOR ME.

Dear Olasha,
You will never believe what has happened. You remember, of course, how the girl, Lily was always impatient with me and called me "peasant." Well, I guess she is impatient with almost everyone, but not with me any longer. And now she calls me Laszlo.

It's all a mystery to me because I have always been fair with her, but let me tell you what happened. We were having our archery class the other day and Lily was partnered with Randall, that bully I told you about.

Anyway, Randall is not as good a shot as Lily and he was particularly bad that day.

So he was angry because he knew that Lily would take great joy in making him look even worse.

And of course she did, which made him none the happier.

I heard her promise him that the next arrow would be a bull's eye. Since I had had a couple of run-ins with Randall myself, I glanced over to see him get some of his own back.

I looked over to catch Randall purposely spoiling Lily's aim. He just couldn't stand to be beaten by a girl and would cheat to prevent it. The cad!

I am certain that I wasn't the only one who saw what happened but when the two of them started to argue no one wanted any part of it.

I'm not sure that I can blame them. Lily isn't the most pleasant student here and Randall would be sure to want revenge. But you know me Lasha, I always want everything to be fair.

And besides, Ghulam had been teaching me some of his wrestling throws and I wasn't afraid of Randall. I know that Lily hadn't been my friend but she didn't deserve to be treated poorly.

You should have seen her face, Lasha. I don't know what she was thinking but I'm sure she didn't expect the "peasant" to come to her rescue.

Characters

WINSTON "FITZ" FITZRANDOLPH

A recognized authority on Victorian era history, Fitz has developed unorthodox ideas which have grown into an obsession. These views ultimately result in his alienation from the academic community and in the disintegration of his personal life. An unexpected assignment sets him on a path that will ultimately vindicate his work or make him realize his folly.

TRASCLAIR "TRACE" BABINEAUX

A New Orleans cab driver and part-time courier for the local mobsters. He claims that he has actually had an encounter with The Victorian and can be found most nights combing the French Quarter seeking locals with a similar experience. In a special code only he can understand, Trace records his findings in a private journal. With his thick Cajun accent, he is often able to charm people into sharing their thoughts with him - though most find his speech amusingly unintelligible.

LEVITICUS "DOC" SHUMPERT

A New Orleans Police detective who is an expert on the occult. A Ph.D., he has spent his entire life writing the definitive study of H.P. Lovecraft. Leviticus wears an eyepatch that he doesn't need. He switches sides frequently, depending on his mood. He believes that by blocking one eye, he can see the world with a slightly different perspective – and it will remind him to question his perceptions and look at something in a new way.

BRANDT SKYLAR "B.S." HARRIMAN

Ray's partner in homicide. The NOPD has its share of eccentric characters, and B.S. is no exception. He combines a near genius I.Q. with a mercilessly sardonic sense of humor. He enjoys playing a game of wits with those around him, but he never shares his innermost thoughts with anyone. He likes to surprise people, so the NOPD can always count on Harriman to show up in the most unusual Mardi Gras costume.

ANDREW JAMES

An Englishman who is an associate of Malcolm Lassiter in the antique business. He travels extensively on buying trips and operates as Lassiter's representative in most transactions and negotiations. James has a rather mysterious past and drops out of sight for periods of time. Elements of international intrigue point to the possibility of James being someone other than the person he appears to be.

CLAUDE BALLARÉ

A gentleman spoken of in hushed tones by those in the New Orleans circle of power and influence. Ballaré is known as someone capable of orchestrating events that will benefit his own fortune. His murky past is no different from dozens of others who have found their way into Louisiana's legion of movers and shakers, but the mystery surrounding his origins has taken on mythic proportions.

Only the Victorian knows Ballaré's true identity and the means he has at hand to carry out his unthinkable plan.

EUDORA KINCAID

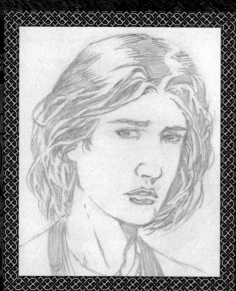

A 17 year old Jamaican immigrant who was orphaned at the age of 8. She lives in New Orleans with her grandmother and other members of her extended family. Eudora attends a Catholic girl's school, but spends most of her time escaping into the colorful world of the French Quarter and documenting what she sees with her treasured camera. Considering her petite size, people are surprised by her fiery and brazen personality.

MALCOLM LASSITER

The owner of Mr. A's Antiques, operating out of the French Quarter. An urbane gentleman who appears well connected to the New Orleans world of power politics and the criminal underground. He is the person who hires Fitz and sends him on a mission to discover the origins of an old bill from the turn of the century - a ten dollar bill that was referred to as the "Jackass note". The most intriguing thing about the bill is not its age, but the fact that it is a near perfect counterfeit.

HAL KELLER

The detective who is Doc's partner. Everyone knows he served in the Special Forces in Vietnam, though he never mentions it – except indirectly when comparing New Orleans to Saigon before the fall, which he does a lot. Known as a genuine cheapskate, Hal will smoke every last crooked cigarette from a damaged carton of Camels.

REYNA "RAY" STARKWEATHER

A homicide detective for the NOPD. "Sam Spade" in female form. Ray sees her life as a film noir movie, with her playing the lead usually reserved for a man. She is all woman and a tough cop. Ray takes her job seriously, which frequently requires her to run interference for her annoying partner, B.S. Harriman.

EDGAR TIPPET

a.k.a. "The Mashed Potato Kid"
A computer science prodigy. He wrote his first computer program at the age of six. He is a consultant to the Mafia, assisting their efforts in cloning software and computers for the black market. He has a nose for shifting power bases and is not too proud to hire out to the highest bidder. Claude Ballaré sees Tippet as an important addition to his elite team.

MISS WHITE

Ballaré's beautiful and fearless enforcer. She exhibits unquestioning loyalty to Ballaré and his mission. Her athletic prowess and powerful mind are well known and respected within Ballaré's organization. She can be irresistibly charming when she needs to be, but don't underestimate the dangerous adversary lurking behind smiling eyes.

Miss White is aware of the Victorian's pursuit of Ballaré and she eagerly anticipates meeting him face to face.

Writing The Victorian has taken me through the rain soaked streets of Houston and down the dark alleyways of the Vieux Carre in New Orleans. It has taken me inside the head of a New England college professor and through the mind of a coked up Rastaman from the welfare slums of New Iberia. Fortunately for me, I didn't walk it alone. Trainor mapped the territory. Marlaine was there to guide me while the wonderful covers by Steranko and Beekman lit the way for us all. Martin and J.C. followed in my footsteps, lifting me up when I needed it and keeping my back covered all the while. Not to be forgotten are Ken, Jim, and Angel for keeping a candle in the window.

– Lovern Kindzierski

It was the worst of times... It was the worst of times...

I sincerely believe that best describes my time before PFP. A lot has changed now, and I think it's for the better so I'd like to acknowledge the crew of PFP for believing in my work, even at times when it left a lot to be desired, and trusting me with their project. A lot of thanks goes especially to Angel for putting up with me day in and day out and to Trainor for encouraging me to always try my best regardless of time constraints. I feel very fortunate to be working with very dedicated people and to be working period. Also to my family for backing me up, especially my dad to whom I owe all my accomplishments, and my girlfriend, Renata, who changed my philosophy that Life Sucks.

Last, but in no way least, the best inker I believe I'll ever have the honor of working with, and good friend J. Carlos Buelna. "Unlike others, please don't let it get to your head."

Gracias!
– Martin
Montiel Luna

First of all, I want to thank Penny-Farthing for giving me the experience of The Victorian—the hospitality of the company has been wonderful and all the people involved in the making of the issues have been great. My friends and family, of course, have been really supportive through the whole thing as well. Also, a very special thanks to my friend Martin, for all the moral support and friendship day after day. I appreciate it more as he keeps giving me better and better work to do.

— J.C. Buelna

Three years ago, when my imagination was doing its usual thing of asking "what if?", I never dreamed that today I would be surrounded by anything that sports a top hat and all things Victorian. Those close to me view this obsession with understanding and those I work with have skillfully fed this condition by applying their immense talents to making this vision come to life. I am forever grateful to Martin, J.C., Lovern and the talented production staff at PFP for patiently listening to my ideas and working tirelessly to make it all happen in each issue.

— Trainor Houghton

A TOAST...
TO YOU GOOD LADIES
AND GENTLEMEN
FOR YOUR UNDYING
SUPPORT...
WE SALUTE YOU.

191

Gallery
Index